A Very Russian Christmas

Roxie Rivera

Night Works Books
College Station, Texas

Roxie Rivera/Night Works Books
3515-B Longmire Dr. #103
College Station, Texas 77845
www.roxierivera.com

Publisher's Note: This is a work of fiction. Names, characters, places, and incidents are a product of the author's imagination. Locales and public names are sometimes used for atmospheric purposes. Any resemblance to actual people, living or dead, or to businesses, companies, events, institutions, or locales is completely coincidental.

A Very Russian Christmas (Her Russian Protector 3.5)/Roxie Rivera. -- 1st ed.
ISBN-10: 1630420093
ISBN-13: 978-1-63042-009-3

DEDICATION

For my family, especially Big O and Little O.

AUTHOR'S NOTE

This collection of holiday themed short stories fits the *Her Russian Protector* series timeline between YURI (Book 3) and the beginning of NIKOLAI (Book 4.) It features couples from the first five books in the series as well as glimpses of future couples to come!

Roxie Rivera

IT'S A WONDERFUL LIFE
DIMITRI

F lat on his back under a crib, Dimitri adjusted one of the corner screws, giving it one final twist, and tested the support system for the mattress. Satisfied that it was just right, he expelled the air from his lungs so he could slide out from under the baby bed. It was a tight fit, and he only barely made it free.

Pushing up off the ground, he took a step back to study the vintage-inspired furniture he had been assembling all afternoon. When he had started the project, he hadn't expected it to be quite so difficult. No one had warned him how tricky these nursery pieces could be to put together. Despite all the frustration, he was glad he had chosen to tackle it today. He couldn't wait to see Benny's face.

Running his hands over the creamy white finish of the beautifully handcrafted crib, he experienced a thrill of anticipation and a flutter of panic. Seeing the first ultrasound of the baby Benny had conceived had been a shocking and utterly profound moment. Having his suspicion that their baby was a girl confirmed last week had been so incredibly moving. Now, touching the crib where their daughter would someday sleep, Dimitri finally felt like this was *really* happening.

I'm going to be a father.

Just two weeks earlier, he had become Benny's husband. He spun his wedding band around his finger and remembered how gorgeous she had looked in her white dress. Making the woman he had loved for so long his wife had been the happiest moment of his life. He harbored no doubts that welcoming their baby in late May was going to be even more joyous.

Clearing away the plastic wrappers and cardboard, Dimitri carted them down to the garage and stuffed them into the recycling and trash bins down there. Back inside the house, he smiled at the way his footsteps echoed in the big, open space. They had closed only that morning so the keys to their new home had been in his hand for less than a day.

Finding the house in Ivan's neighborhood had been a stroke of luck. Houses didn't come up for sale very often in the area and the few that did weren't available for long because the area was so popular with its oversized lots and large homes. He had been on his way to inspect one of the few remaining lots in the neighborhood when he had spotted a real estate agent hammering a sign into the front yard of this house just one street away from Ivan and Erin. He had pulled over immediately to chat with the realtor, texted Benny some quick snapshots while touring the house and made an offer the moment she confirmed she loved it.

And now it belonged to them.

Glancing around the spacious downstairs, he mentally

catalogued the upgrades and small remodeling projects they wanted to have done. The carpet had to go first. He already had an appointment with a flooring store that Ivan had recommended. The walls needed new paint— especially that garish orange in the kitchen. The chandelier in the dining room and the one above the stairs had to be replaced with something that fit their style instead of the dungeon-like metal with faux candles.

Tomorrow morning, he would start putting out feelers for contractors to tackle the bigger projects. Some of the work he would do himself, but with his company's recent launch and the sheer number of hours he had to work to get it off the ground, hiring out most of the labor was the best idea.

He leaned back against the nearest wall and simply took a moment to appreciate everything he had accomplished. As an orphaned child who had lived hand-to-mouth, he had dreamed of new clothes, a full belly and a warm bed. Small, realistic goals were smart and attainable—but this? This was beyond his wildest dreams.

To know that he could provide such a home for his wife and child filled Dimitri with the strongest sense of pride. Everything he had fought to survive and surmount after his hard start in life had brought him to this point— and he had never been happier.

Rattling keys outside the front door drew his attention. He crossed the living area and turned into the entryway just as the door opened and Benny stepped inside. She seemed startled by his presence. "Dima!"

He still smiled every time she used his childhood nickname. When they had married, Yuri, one of his closest friends, had insisted that Benny start using it. "Sweetheart, what are you doing here?"

"Um…I guess I should ask you the same thing."

He didn't want to spoil the surprise. "I thought I'd come over and start making a list of the projects for the house. What are you doing here?"

"I had hoped to get here before you so I could surprise you with dinner and a sort of camping setup in our bedroom so we could spent the night here."

Touched by her thoughtfulness, he joined her at the door. Glancing around her, he spotted the small pile of store bags and a suitcase. When he lifted the sack holding an air mattress, he frowned and gently scolded his wife. "Benny, you shouldn't be lifting such heavy things. A gallon of milk, remember? You promised nothing heavier than that."

She bit her full bottom lip. "Well…it wasn't that much heavier."

He shot her a look as he carted everything into the entryway and shut the door behind her, sealing out the cold December chill. Cupping her chin, he forced Benny to meet his gaze. "I appreciate the surprise very much, but it wouldn't have been much fun if you had hurt yourself."

Hoping his words didn't carry the sting of censure, he leaned down to capture her mouth in a tender kiss. Benny's gloved hands glided up his arms and rested on his biceps. She tasted of hot cocoa and those fluffy, minty marshmallows her bakery made fresh every morning during the holiday season. Pulling back, he smiled down at her. "I hope you brought some marshmallows for me."

"I did."

"Good." He tapped the tip of her nose before untangling himself from their embrace. "I'll get everything set up in the master bedroom while you fix dinner."

Nodding, she grabbed the bags she needed and disappeared into the kitchen. He gathered up the suitcase and bedding supplies and carted everything upstairs. His armful was bulky and unwieldy, but he figured it was good practice for the coming days when he would be juggling a stroller, car seat, diaper bag and baby.

By the time he had everything situated, Benny was calling up to him from the bottom of the stairs. He discovered her in the kitchen standing next to one of the bar stools that had been left by the prior owners. She eyed the tall chair with the oddly patterned upholstery with a mistrusting eye. "What's wrong?"

"There's no way my pregnant behind is getting up there."

Laughing, he agreed with her assessment. "Not without some help." He lifted her up, deposited her on the seat and pecked her cheek. "See? I have my uses."

"You just love to show off those big, sexy muscles of yours."

"Only for you, baby." He slid onto the stool next to her. "Only for you."

She snorted lightly and reached for one of the takeout containers from his favorite Italian restaurant. "Ogling those yummy muscles of yours is what got me into this predicament." She pointed to her round belly with a plastic fork. "I'm hoping that I'll be immune to your hotness by the time she's born. Otherwise I'm going to find myself right back in this position."

"There are a couple of positions I'd love to have you in tonight." He shot her a smoldering look that made her cheeks heat up with redness. Even after all the months they had been lovers, she still blushed so easily—and he found it incredibly enticing and endearing.

"I can't believe you're turned on by all this." She shook her head as she gestured to her pregnant belly and firm, heavy breasts. "I'm starting to look like a science experiment gone awry."

Putting down his fork, he slid his arm along the back of her chair and cupped her face with his other hand. Staring into her eyes, he made sure to use a firm tone to get his point across. "You are the sexiest fucking woman I have ever known." His hand drifted down to the high, round curve of her belly. "I love the way you look now. You're giving me the most amazing gift. How can I not love that? And think of how sensitive you are now."

She gulped as his hand moved from her belly to her breast and along the edge of her neck. Was she remembering the way he had taken her last night, her thighs splayed wide open as he pounded into her from behind and tugged on her hair in the way that made her so hot? One flick of his fingers against her clit, and she had come so hard and so loud he had feared the neighbors would call the police.

"Look at me," he urged. "Do I need to strip you down right now and show you how much I want you?"

She licked her lips and shook her head. "I believe you."

He kissed her, flicking his tongue against hers until she shivered in his arms and leaned against him for support. Certain she did believe him, he eased off the kiss and pressed his lips to her temple. "I love you, Benny. Pregnant, not pregnant, young, old—you're it for me. You're the only woman I want."

"You're the only one I want too." She peppered light kisses along his jaw and cheek. "I really love you."

"I know you do, *milaya moya*." Sliding back to his seat, he motioned to her empty plate. "Eat. I'm sure our daughter will be kicking soon if you don't feed her."

Since Benny had first experienced movement earlier in the month, they had noticed that the baby seemed to kick the most when Benny was between meals and snacks. The baby was already big for her age, but so far Benny had shown no indication of gestational diabetes that was often the cause for babies measuring ahead. Of course, one look at him and their obstetrician had chalked it up to his larger than average frame. It seemed their daughter wouldn't be taking after her petite mama.

"I packed my laptop in case we want to watch a movie or something later," Benny said as she cleared away the island where they had eaten. She stowed the leftovers in the refrigerator and ran her hands over the gleaming stainless steel exterior. "We got lucky with the kitchen appliances. This collection is fantastic."

Pleased by her approval, he crossed that off the list he was running in his head. "If we keep the appliances, there will be more cash in the budget for the other projects you wanted to do in here."

"I'm perfectly happy to keep these." She wrinkled that dainty nose while glaring at the orange walls. "But these walls! They have to go."

"Do you know what color you would like to use?"

"I have a vague idea of something in a pale gray."

His brow furrowed. "Gray?"

She put a hand on her hip. "Yes. Gray. Why?"

Choosing his battles, Dimitri shrugged. "If you think gray will be nice, then I'll grab some gray paint chips on the way home tomorrow."

"Just like that, huh? No argument?"

"No argument." He bent down and kissed her. "The kitchen is your domain. You can paint it purple with lime green stripes for all I care."

"And your domain?"

"The garage, I suspect," he said with a laugh. "I hear that's where most of my married friends end up spending most of their time."

She rolled her eyes. "If you want a man-cave, pick out one of the extra rooms upstairs. We'll only be using the master suite and the nursery next door. That leaves three extra rooms."

"Until Natalya has a brother," he said, placing a protective hand on her baby bump. "And then a sister and another brother and—"

"Are you nuts?" she asked amid laughter. "Let's just start with one and see how that goes."

"All right, *lyubimaya*. We'll start with one."

"And her name is Sofia," she reminded him.

"That's not a battle you're going to win as easily as the paint color for the kitchen," he lightly warned. "I like Natalya. It's a beautiful name."

"So is Sofia."

Ending their argument with a gentle kiss, he said, "There's plenty of time for us to fight about that. Come upstairs with me. I want to show you something."

Hand in hand, he led her to the room they had chosen as their nursery and tugged her along behind him. When he stepped aside, she spotted the furniture. "Dimitri!"

"I know we have to take out the carpet and paint the walls but I wanted you to see our baby's furniture here. I wanted you to see how wonderful it's going to be."

Benny smiled at him and made her way to the crib. She touched the pretty finish. "How did you know this was the set I wanted?"

"I found the catalog you had hidden under the stack of magazines next to the bed."

"It was really expensive, Dima."

"So we'll make cuts elsewhere in the budget," he said. "We'll make it work."

"We always do."

"Yes." He thought of all the things they survived and accomplished together. "Perhaps that should be our family motto."

Benny crossed the distance between them and wound her arms around his waist. When she peered up at him, the depth of her love for him was reflected in her eyes. "I know we're only just getting started, Dimitri, but I think we're going to have a wonderful life together."

"We are," he hurriedly agreed. "It's going to be so good for us, Benny. I'm sure there will be lean times between our two businesses, but we're smart and careful. We'll get through them." He cupped her nape and nuzzled their mouths together. "I keep thinking that I couldn't possibly be any happier with you and then something new and wonderful happens like the baby and now the house."

"You're the one who made all that possible." She rose on tiptoes to claim his mouth. "You're the one who gave me this baby and this house and saved my business."

"I'll give you so much more, Benny." He swore the words like a vow. "You can count on me. I'll work harder than any man to make sure you and the children have everything you need and want."

"We only need you, Dimitri. Just you." She brought his hand down to her belly and slipped it under her shirt. Though she had been able to feel movement for weeks, he hadn't been so lucky.

Until now.

A surprisingly powerful kick tapped his palm. His eyes widened and his jaw dropped at the alien sensation. Wondering if he had truly felt his daughter, he was quickly assured that he had when she kicked at his hand again. Prickly heat irritated his eyes, and he blinked rapidly. "I feel her!"

"She's pretty amazing, huh?"

"So amazing." He followed the baby's movements, pressing gently to coax more kicks from her and laughing when little Natalya responded. Fascinated by the tender moment, he asked, "What does it feel like for you?"

"It's strange," Benny admitted. "But it's so incredible to have her with me all the time. When she moves, I know she's happy and healthy. It's reassuring."

"I'm actually jealous," he confessed with a short laugh. Sliding to his knees, Dimitri pushed Benny's shirt out of the way and dotted loving kisses across her belly. The sweetness of their family moment faded, and Dimitri's kisses grew sensual.

She ran her fingers through his thick hair. "Dimitri?"

"We have a bed right next door."

"Yes. And?"

"And I think it's time we break in the new house." Standing up, he swept his wife up into his arms, grinning at her squeal of laughter, and carried her into their master bedroom. The air mattress was far from the comfort of their king-sized bed, but it would be fun for one night.

"It's like making love in a bouncy castle," Benny joked as Dimitri climbed onto the mattress with her.

"A what?"

"A bouncy castle," she repeated. "One of those big, inflatable castles that parents rent for a kid's party."

He stopped stripping her just long enough to catch her gaze. "We have to rent a castle for Natalya's birthday?"

"Definitely," she said, lifting her hips so he could tug her jeans free. "Knowing the way you're going to spoil her, *Sofia*," she emphasized the name, "will probably convince you to hire a petting zoo and a magician and—"

"God, I really need to get some more wealthy clients at the security firm," Dimitri grumbled while peeling away

Benny's shirt and expertly unhooking her bra. "*Natalya's* first birthday party is going to cost more than a year at university."

"Not if you learn to tell her no," Benny suggested.

Sliding down onto his stomach, Dimitri grasped her panties and jerked them down her hips. "I can't even tell her mother no."

Giggling, Benny wiggled her hips until her cotton underpants were out of the way. He tossed them over his shoulder and insinuated himself between her thighs. Draping her legs over his shoulders, Dimitri rubbed his lips side to side across the seam of his wife's pussy before using his fingers to part her delicate folds. With her clitoris revealed to him, he wasted no time giving Benny exactly what she wanted.

"Oh, Dima," she breathed his nickname on a rapturous sigh. His tongue swirled around the little pearl hidden there, coaxing it free from its hood and rewarding the tiny nub with soft flicks. Because she was so sensitive, Benny didn't need much stimulation to reach a climax these days, but eating her pussy was one of his favorite things so he took his time lavishing her with oral attention.

Hips rocking and toes curling against his tattooed back, Benny whispered his name over and over. He dipped his tongue into the slick entrance of her before gliding it back to that swollen kernel and concentrating all his efforts there. With focused swipes, he pushed Benny higher and higher until finally, he suckled her clitoris and fluttered his tongue over it.

"*Ah!*" Head thrown back and hips snapping wildly, Benny pushed her pussy firmly against his mouth and rode the blissful waves of her climax. Loving the sound of her going crazy with pleasure, he drew it out as long as possible, only pulling back when she dropped down to the mattress and whimpered.

Wiping his mouth with the back of his hand, Dimitri slid down next to her, rolled onto his back and dragged her on top of him. Heavy with his baby, Benny presented the most erotic vision as she straddled his legs. Grasping her bottom in one hand and his thick cock in the other, he pressed the head of it between her plump, wet labia until he was right where he wanted to be.

He gently thrust up into his wife, always mindful of her comfort, and watched her face for signs that she needed him to adjust his tactics. Her smoky eyes closed briefly, and she bit her lip. "You feel so good, Dimitri."

Palming her breast, he circled her sensitive nipple with his thumb and urged her to ride him. "Make me come, Benny."

Hands on his chest, she worked her hips back and forth and swiveled until she found a pace that made them both groan. He caressed her breasts, taking care not to pinch her nipples too hard, and then settled his hands on that luscious ass. He guided her movements, telling her with a squeeze and a playful swat just how fast and hard he wanted it.

A pulsing, throbbing heat started low in his belly. A slight buzz traveled through his legs. Balls tight, he clamped down on his building orgasm, hoping to hold off just long enough for Benny to find her release. He licked his thumb and placed the wide digit just to the side of her stiff clit.

With a little strumming motion, Benny shattered atop him, her entire body quaking as she climaxed long and hard. The fluttering squeeze of her pussy was all it took to make him lose control. Unleashing the tether on his own release, Dimitri let the spasms of her cunt milk him dry.

She fell forward, and he gathered her in his arms. Ever so carefully, he placed her on her side and dragged the quilt up over their naked bodies. Side by side, they smiled, kissed and petted until Benny finally succumbed to the exhaustion of another long day. Not quite ready to fall asleep, he was content to stroke her hair and hold her close.

For a long time, he simply stared down at the dark-haired vixen he had loved from afar for so long. Sometimes he couldn't believe that only a few short months ago, he had feared she would never see him as anything other than her friend. Now she carried his last name and his child. It didn't seem possible that any man should be so lucky, but he was.

He was the luckiest man in the world.

You can read about Benny and Dimitri's romance in DIMITRI (Her Russian Protector #2) available now in ebook and in print. An audiobook version will be available in early 2014.

A LUXURY SLEIGH RIDE
ALEXEI

S tretching his aching neck, Alexei Sarnov crossed his office while waiting for Nikolai to answer his call. He made his way to the glass wall that allowed him to look down into the bullpen of car salesman at his flagship luxury dealership. This late on Christmas Eve, there were just a handful of his employees puttering around the place, most of them wrapping up delivery details for Christmas morning surprises.

"Alexei!" Festive music blared in the background but grew softer as Nikolai seemed to dart into a quiet area at his restaurant.

He smiled at Nikolai's warm greeting. "How are you?"

"Very well, and you?"

"I can't complain." With the year shaping up to be the very best since he had opened, Alexei honestly couldn't. "I'm sure you're busy with the Samovar Christmas party but I wanted to make sure the car delivered earlier met your standards?"

Last week, his former boss had come to the dealership

looking for a car for the waitress and artist he regarded as his ward. Alexei suspected there was more than simple platonic affection between them but he would never voice those thoughts aloud. Nikolai might not be his boss anymore but he was still an incredibly powerful and dangerous man, the sort Alexei absolutely did not want as an enemy.

"It's perfect, Alexei. I'm sure she's going to be thrilled. You did extremely well."

"I'm glad you're happy." *I'm relieved, actually*, he thought to himself. Nikolai wasn't an easy man to please but he had been more than fair in their dealings, not once trying to get any type of *family* discount. He had paid sticker price for the luxury coupe and simply asked that it be delivered with a bright red bow. "Please let me know if there is anything else I can do for you."

"The same goes for you, Alexei."

As the call ended, he spotted their nightly janitorial crew making their way from the back rooms to the main floor of the dealership. He tucked his phone into his pocket and watched the two sisters push their carts. The older sister was always on her phone while she worked and tonight was no exception. God only knew what she had to talk about this late at night. Apparently she was very popular.

The other sister, the younger one, went about her routine in the way he had come to expect. Industrious and quiet, Shay Sandoval started at the far left side of the building and began her methodical approach toward the center. He had watched her clean enough nights to know that Shay would eventually end up picking up the slack on her sister's side too. Something told him she had been picking up her sister's slack for years.

Turning away from the wall, he headed back to his

desk and tackled the day's paperwork. He was drumming his fingers and wondering how best to incentivize his sales staff in the New Year when a timid knock against his door interrupted him. "*Da*? Yes?"

Shay cautiously poked her head into his office. "Um…Mr. Sarnov? Would you like me to tidy up in here? Your door has been locked the last few nights and I haven't had a chance to clean."

He waved her inside. "Please."

With a nod of her head, she carted in a shallow tote stocked with cleaning products and tools. Making little noise, she started tidying up his office. He thought about striking up a conversation with her but realized he didn't know much about Shay other than her name and the length of time she had worked at the janitorial company.

"I'm sure you can't wait to get home to celebrate the holidays." He figured that was a safe enough bet.

"Sure," she said, her voice soft and nervous. "And you?"

He shrugged and leaned back in his chair. "I don't have much to celebrate."

She shot him a strange look. "Really? You seem to have quite an amazing life."

"Do I?" He wondered what she knew of his life.

Holding a duster, she swallowed. "Well…I mean…from what I can see. Your businesses are extremely successful. You're well-respected in the community."

"Yes." He didn't deny those things. After coming to Houston as part of Nikolai Kalasnikov's hand-picked crew, he had earned his nest egg fighting in cages for the boss. His loyalty to Nikolai had been rewarded with this dealership. Six years later, Alexei owned a string of luxury and mid-range dealerships in the Houston area and a trucking company. "I've been incredibly lucky."

She shook her head and turned back to the bookshelves. Rising up on tiptoes, she dragged the duster along the exposed edges. "I don't think it was luck. I think it was hard work and determination."

He wasn't used to receiving such compliments. "Thank you."

Unable to help himself, Alexei tilted his head and focused his gaze on that pert little ass of hers. She wore bright pink scrubs embroidered with the janitorial company's logo and a long-sleeved Henley style top underneath. Despite the boxy cut of the outfit, he got a very nice look at her nubile form anytime she stretched.

Dragging his gaze away from her bottom, he turned back to his computer screen and tried to focus on the monthly sales figures in front of him. He wondered at his reaction to Shay. She wasn't anything like the women who usually caught his eye.

With that sleek black hair she wore in a high ponytail and her warm brown skin, she was the complete opposite of the blondes and brunettes he typically dated. Well—dated was too strong a word for the arrangements he preferred. He had long ago discovered that keeping a mistress worked best for his particular needs.

His mind strayed to the idea of Shay in that sort of role. Almost immediately, he realized it wouldn't work. She was college-aged, twenty-two or twenty-three, and much too young for that sort of thing. He preferred an older woman, the sort who understood the score and had enough skill and tricks to keep him satisfied in the bedroom. He liked women who were experienced enough to understand that they could never ask for more than he was willing to give.

Money, a luxurious apartment, shopping sprees, a new

car and jewelry—he heaped those on his kept women, but when he tired of them, he expected them to move along without causing a fuss. A few had attempted to wheedle their way back into his bed, but he never allowed it. When he was done, he was done. No woman had ever succeeded in capturing his heart...and no woman ever would.

"Mr. Sarnov?" Shay's gentle voice dragged him from his thoughts. She stood near his desk with a microfiber towel in hand.

"I'm sorry. What did you say?"

"I asked if you wanted me to clean your desk."

"Oh." He sat back and pushed out of his chair. "Yes."

When he rose to his full height, she took a quick step back and glanced up at him with surprise. A big man who had fought on the underground bare-knuckle circuit for years, he was used to intimidating people. He got the feeling it wasn't his size that frightened her as much as the tattoos on his hands.

Since leaving that mob life behind, he had taken great pains to learn to fit in and blend. He wore long sleeves and stuck to buttoned shirts and ties when handling his business affairs to make sure most of his tattoos were covered. Once, he had even considered having the ones on his hands lasered away, but something had stopped him from following through with the procedure. It seemed dishonest and fake to blast away the reminders of the life he had once embraced—and the life he had fought like hell to escape. Right or wrong, he had earned every single one of those marks.

Noticing the way she gripped the towel in her hand, Alexei decided to clear out of his office while she worked. "Let me know when you're done."

"I will."

Heading downstairs, he tried to ignore the tight ache in his chest at the realization that she was afraid of him. He couldn't pinpoint the exact reason it bothered him. It wasn't until he was chatting with his general manager Martha that he realized why Shay's reaction left him feeling raw and agitated. That fearful, mistrusting glint in her dark eyes? It told him that she had been hit. The way she had zeroed in on his inked hands assured him it had been a man with tattoos.

After walking Martha to the door and bidding her a good night and happy holiday, he turned back toward the main sales floor and glanced up at his office. His teeth clenched at the very idea of some asshole putting his hands on Shay. The thought of someone striking such a sweet, gentle woman just burned him up.

The sister caught his eye. Still twittering away into her phone, Shannon half-heartedly pushed a broom from one end of the building to the other. Martha had complained about her once or twice, but the janitorial service assured him that Shannon and Shay had the highest customer satisfaction ratings among their clients. No doubt Shay's attention to detail was the reason for those high marks.

Dedicated and diligent, she had already finished his office and was working her way through the finance and inventory offices next to his. Alexei found things to keep him busy and away from her by ducking into the service garages out back. When he returned, he found Shay moving down the staircase, wiping the hand rails and steps until they gleamed.

He tried not to stare at the wiggling motion of her bottom but he wasn't a damned eunuch. He was a red-blooded man with needs and that shaking ass of hers was pushing him toward a line he refused to cross. He didn't fuck employees, and he sure as hell didn't get involved with sweet young things like that.

That's why he had women like Marissa at his beck and call. It was simpler that way, with no strings and no expectations. He could pop over to the apartment he kept for his women, have a few hours of fun and then get the hell out and go home. There were no awkward morning run-ins and no guilt trips.

He waited until Shay had moved into the break room to return to his office. Pushing her out of his mind, he called out to the security station and had the two night guards close and lock up the gates. They would need to be opened when the last few employees in the service garages out back left and when Shay and her sister were ready to leave, but he didn't want anyone else getting onto the lot.

Lost in his work, he didn't notice another hour had passed until Shay knocked on his door again. She held a clipboard and teethed her lower lip. "Mr. Sarnov? Dan, your maintenance guy, usually signs these slips for us, but he's not here tonight. Would you mind?"

"Sure." He gestured for her to bring him the slip. Their fingers brushed together, hers slightly cold, when she handed over the paper. He ignored the way the simple act of touching her made his stomach leap and the way she snatched back her hand.

"I know the floors are usually waxed on Sundays, but they look really dim. You might want to call in and have them send Manny out to do them on Thursday or Friday, especially if you think you're going to have an increase in foot traffic after Christmas tomorrow."

Surprised by her thoughtful suggestion, he nodded. "I'll do that. Thank you."

She shrugged. "I'm just passing along what I noticed."

"I appreciate it."

"Is that hard?" She asked as he signed his name across the bottom of the work ticket.

"Is what hard?" He had to stop himself from tacking on a pet name at the end. The tip of his tongue burned with the unused *sweetheart* she unwittingly inspired.

"Using two different alphabets," she explained, taking the ticket from him.

"Oh." He tossed aside his pen and shook his head. "You get used to it."

She tapped the notepad on his desk and ran her finger over the Cyrillic script. "But you still make notes to yourself in Russian?"

"Old habits," he murmured, wondering at the way she noticed all the little things he did. "What about you? Do you speak another language?"

"Spanish," she said. "My dad taught me."

He sensed there was more of a story there but didn't push. He had noticed that Shay had darker coloring than her fair-haired, light-skinned sister. They obviously hadn't had the same father, but that was hardly the sort of thing that was any of his business.

Hearing the soft splatter of icy sleet against the window behind him, he asked, "Do you have another job after this one?"

Her brow furrowed. "You mean another cleaning job? No. Not tonight. You're our only stop."

The way she answered piqued his interest. "You work somewhere else?"

She nodded. "I wait tables at an all-night diner near one of the refineries a few nights a week."

"But you're on swing shift with the janitorial company, yes?"

"Yes."

He quickly calculated the hours she worked. The

number he arrived at displeased him. "Aren't you in school?"

"Three days a week," she said, a small frown playing upon her lips.

"And you get enough rest for that? You must be working fifty hours a week."

"School is expensive and landlords don't just let you live in their homes for free." Signaling an end to the discussion, she smiled at him and backed away from his desk. "Good night, Mr. Sarnov. Merry Christmas."

"Merry Christmas." He watched her leave, all the while wondering why the hell she had gotten under his skin tonight. Certain it was the temptation of the forbidden that called to him, Alexei convinced himself that a nice romp with Marissa would cure him of whatever lingering interest remained. He picked up his phone to let her know that he would be stopping by the apartment later but decided against it. She knew the rules of their arrangement, and he wasn't required to give her anything more than half an hour's notice before his arrival.

Fully aware that he was testing Marissa, Alexei set aside his phone and finished tying up the loose ends of his work. He didn't know how much longer he would keep Marissa. It had been nearly five months—and that was pushing the boundaries for him. She had started to get comfortable and had even attempted to make demands on his time.

Perhaps it was time to head over to one of Kostya's clubs and take a look at the new dancers. He had had good luck in the past plucking a mistress right off the pole and depositing her in the apartment he kept. Those women were smart enough to negotiate going into the arrangement to get the best deal for themselves, and he liked that. If they were both using one another for what they wanted, it didn't feel nearly as dirty.

After locking up his office, he slid into his wool coat and hit the button on his key fob for the remote start to his vehicle. He wanted it nice and warm when he slid behind the wheel. He moved through the building to turn out the lights and stopped at the main entrance to punch in the code for the security system. He heard his phone ringing in his office but ignored it. Whoever it was would leave a message.

Out in the cold December night, he started toward his vehicle. The weather forecast had been bad that morning so he had driven his SUV instead of his sports car. He hadn't made it six steps before he heard the thump of a car stereo's bass. The hip hop beat wasn't totally unexpected, and he initially assumed it was one of the mechanics heading home for the night—until he heard the unmistakable sound of Shay's raised voice.

Hackles raised, Alexei strode down the sidewalk and around the corner of the building to the employee parking lot. He spotted the small white car Shay and her sister drove, the hood of it popped and the engine steaming. A few rows back in the empty lot sat a black SUV with ridiculous gold rims and music blaring so loudly the fucking glass was shaking. He had a mind to call the security guards to see who had let them onto the lot but then remembered the phone call he had just dodged. No doubt the guards had made a decision when he hadn't answered. It was the wrong one.

With the experience of many years living in the underworld and even now existing right on the fringe of it, Alexei sized up the scene before him with speed. There were at least two other men inside the SUV and two of them standing outside it, one of them with his arm draped around Shannon. Shay stood close to the white car, arms crossed as she shook her head and argued with her sister. Over what he couldn't say but Shay's body language was clear to him. She didn't want to get in that Escalade—and he sure as hell wasn't going to let her.

Quickly tugging on the knot of his silk tie, he ripped it free and stuffed it into the pocket of his coat before flicking open the top buttons of his shirt. With the collar wide open and the fabric gaping, the heavy prison and mob ink he usually kept hidden was on clear display. From this distance, he couldn't be sure if the men from the SUV were affiliated with a gang or not, but he figured they would have no problem recognizing the ink emblazoned on his skin if they were. If they weren't, it would scare the shit out of them.

"Shay?" He raised his voice as he stalked toward her. "Is there a problem?"

Embarrassment flashed across her pretty face. She gestured toward the broken-down vehicle. "Our car is having problems."

"I can see that." He moved close to her, standing near enough that he could grab Shay and throw her behind him if it got violent. Holding the gaze of the man who had laid claim to Shannon, he asked, "Do you think that music is loud enough?"

The man glanced at his car and flicked his fingers, the movement giving Alexei a clear view of the gang sign tattooed on the guy's neck. He recognized the mark of the Guzman cartel and deduced this was one of their street-level pushers. The dealer held up a hand. "No hard feelings, *mano*. We were just about to leave as soon my girl gets her sister in line."

"Come on, Shay." Shannon was all smiles as she pleaded with her sister, but he wasn't fooled. "Ruben came all the way out here to get us so we can go to this

Christmas party. It'll be fun—and Lalo really wants to meet you!"

Lalo? Alexei might have been out of the street life but he kept his ear to the ground and knew all about Eduardo "Lalo" Contreras. He was the top enforcer for the cartel here in Houston. There was no way in hell he was letting Shay get mixed up with that man.

Not breaking his gaze with the dealer, Alexei extended his arm to prevent Shay from taking even one single step. "Shay, get your things. I'll take you home." He glanced at Shannon. "If you would like a ride, I'm happy to take you."

Shannon frowned at him. "No, thanks. I actually like to have fun—unlike some people."

Shay didn't take the bait. She turned back toward the car and gathered up her things.

The boyfriend dropped his arm from Shannon's shoulders and took a cautious step forward. He had a conciliatory air about him. "*Oye, mano*, I didn't know that she was your girl. I'll make sure Lalo knows that she's on the Red team. We won't bother her again."

Shay wasn't his girl and she wasn't playing for the Russian team, but Alexei wasn't about to correct the gangbanger's misconceptions. It was safer for Shay if the cartel crews in town thought she was safely tucked under the umbrella of Nikolai's guardianship. "I would appreciate that."

The boyfriend nodded and hustled Shannon into the middle row of seats. Alexei stood back and watched the SUV drive away before turning his attention to Shay. With a backpack on one shoulder and her purse clenched in the other, she chewed her lower lip and looked like she might burst into tears at any moment.

"Hey," he said gently and came to stand in front of

her. "It's all right. Those men can't hurt you."

"I am so sorry."

"For what?"

"For dragging you into that messy situation," she explained in a voice wavering with anxiety.

"You didn't drag me into anything. I could have walked away or ignored it."

She fidgeted with the handle of her leather purse. "Why didn't you?"

"Because I've been around long enough to spot trouble," he said, taking a look at the engine. It seemed to be a straightforward radiator problem. Closing the hood, he promised, "I'll have the guys in the garage take a look at this as soon as possible. We'll get you a rental car until it's finished."

"Oh, um, I don't think my car insurance will cover it."

"Then it will be my Christmas gift."

"No, Mr. Sarnov, you don't have to do that."

Fighting the urge to reach out and caress her cheek, he replied, "It's Christmas. Let me do something nice for you." He motioned toward the building. "Come on. Let's get you home. It's freezing out here."

Not letting her protest the gift, he placed his hand against the puffy back of her jacket and gently pressed her forward. When they reached his SUV, Shay seemed taken aback by the simple action of opening and closing her door. He couldn't help but wonder what sort of men she was dating if a man opening her door was such a surprise. The wrong ones, he surmised as he slid behind the wheel.

"Punch in your address." He pointed to the navigation screen mounted to the dash. "Do you need to stop anywhere before I drop you off?"

"No."

"You're sure?" He fastened his seatbelt as she tapped

at the screen. "It will be nine or ten in the morning before I'm able to get a rental car to your house. If there's any errands you need to run, I'll take you tonight."

"I did all of the grocery shopping earlier this week. I'm good but thank you. For everything," she added with a smile that dazzled him.

He tried to ignore the stirring of attraction and focused on the map that popped up in front of him. The area where she lived wasn't a very nice one, but he kept his opinion to himself. God only knew he had lived in some terrible places during his life. Even so, he didn't like the idea of Shay and her sister living alone there. It was a neighborhood that was constantly on the news because of drug and gun raids and worse.

They drove in silence at first. As they idled at a light, he noticed the way Shay clutched her purse. The white-knuckle grip disturbed him, especially when he remembered the way she had reacted to him standing over her in his office. "Are you that afraid to be alone with me?"

"What?" Her gaze snapped to his face. "I'm not afraid of you."

"No?" He glanced at her hands. "Then why—?"

"It's the weather," she interrupted. "I don't like icy roads. They make me nervous."

"It's hardly icy. They haven't even needed to sand the roads yet."

"Yeah, well, I'm sure that's what my dad was thinking when he got in his truck to go to work the night he died."

He silently cursed himself for the flippant reply. "I'm sorry about your father. Was it very recent?"

"No. I was only seven when he died."

Mindful of her fear, he eased on the gas when the light turned green and drove more cautiously so as not to upset her. "What about your mother? Is she still alive?"

"I guess."

"You guess?" He glanced at her. "How do you not know if your mother is alive or dead?"

"She walked out on us when Shannon turned seventeen. Just…left." Her grip loosened on her purse, and she shifted in her seat so she had a better line of sight on him. "I know you probably think Shannon was really irresponsible back there, but she had to give up a lot to help raise me after Mom split. She deserves to go out and have fun every now and then."

"Not with men like that," he interjected gruffly. "You were smart enough to know not to get in that vehicle."

"It wasn't Ruben and his friends who scared me. I grew up with most of them."

"What scared you?" He already knew the answer but wanted to hear it from her lips.

"Lalo Contreras."

"The drug dealer."

She nodded. "The drug dealer."

"He's interested in you?" He hated the sharp edge to his voice. Jealousy wasn't an emotion he was used to feeling. Why the hell was it zipping through him now?

"Unfortunately," she said softly. "I made the mistake of letting Shannon convince me to go out to a Halloween party with her. He was the host, and I guess I caught his eye."

Alexei didn't find that the least bit surprising. He could only imagine how tempting she would have looked in a sexy little Halloween costume. The vision of her in a naughty French maid's outfit sent a white-hot blaze of heat right through him. Hoping to cool his raging lust, he turned to more serious issues. "You should stay away from men like that."

"I have no intention of getting caught up with a man like Lalo."

"Good."

She didn't speak again until they were sitting at another red light. "I didn't mean to make you uncomfortable earlier in your office."

"Uncomfortable?"

"When you stood up, I mean."

"Oh. That."

"Yeah, it's not you. Really," she added quickly. "It's just—I saw the tattoos on your hand, and I had this weird flashback to uglier times."

"A boyfriend?"

"Not my boyfriend," she murmured and turned to look out the window.

The way she said it slashed at him. He kept his gaze focused on the windshield and the crystallized droplets hitting the glass and melting almost instantly. "Your mother's boyfriend?"

She waited a moment to answer. "Yes."

His fingers tightened around the steering wheel until his fingers were numb. "Did he—?"

"No," she hastily interjected. "He never touched me like *that*."

He exhaled a pent-up breath. "But he hit you."

"Yes."

Glancing at her, he took in the silhouette of her face. The red brake lights and the shimmering Christmas lights decorating the building on the corner illuminated her honey brown skin. A warm sensation invaded his chest. "Do you want me to track him down and hit him a few times?"

She snorted with amusement and smiled at him. "No, but thanks."

"You're sure? I wouldn't mind. Hell, it might be fun."

"I'm sure." Her gaze moved to his hands. "You were a fighter, right?"

"Yes."

"Underground?"

"Yes. How did you know?"

"People talk."

He didn't even want to think about what people said about him behind his back. "That was a long time ago. I'm not that man anymore."

"Do you miss it?"

"The fighting? Sometimes," he admitted. "It's the other part—"

"The mob?" she bravely asked.

His gaze flicked from the road to her face and back again. She was the first woman who had ever come right out and asked about his past. "Yes. That's the part I don't miss."

"For what it's worth, I think that the life you've built for yourself is amazing. You should be extremely proud of what you've accomplished."

He swallowed hard and couldn't meet her gaze. The kindness of her remark unsettled him. "Thank you."

They fell into a comfortable, easy silence for the remainder of the drive. When he pulled into the mobile home park where she lived, the navigation instructions ended. She pointed out a left turn and then a right into the narrow gravel driveway.

He eyed the single-wide mobile home with its faded blue shutters. The SUV he drove probably cost two or three times as much as her home. Even so, the yard was immaculately neat. Simple white Christmas lights decorated the porch where potted poinsettias lined the steps. A festive wreath adorned the door.

Unlatching his seatbelt, he said, "I'll walk you inside."

She shot him a bemused look. "Why?"

"Because you're alone and this neighborhood is—," he caught himself before he said something that would hurt her feelings, "—very dark. You can never be too cautious."

"Well…okay." She hopped out of the front seat before he could make it around to her side. His lips settled into an irritated line as he shut the door and followed her up the sidewalk and onto the porch. The fact that she didn't expect a man to do nice things for her annoyed him. Didn't she realize she was worth that and so much more?

The enticing scent of cinnamon and the warmth of the house were so inviting. He shut the storm door behind him and hesitated just inside the threshold. He had seen her safely inside. It was time to go.

But he couldn't make his feet move.

"Would you like some coffee or tea?"

"Tea, please."

"It'll be a few minutes. Please make yourself comfortable."

After shrugging out of her jacket, she dropped her bags on a couch that had seen much better days. He wasn't fooled by the throw blanket draped over the back or the plush pillows artfully arranged to hide the worn upholstery. The shade of the carpet—a forest green—wasn't one he had ever seen anywhere else, but it seemed to match the accents on the walls that looked original to the trailer.

Despite the age of the home, it was clear that Shay and her sister had taken very good care of it and had pride in their small space. Everything was super clean and neat. The photos on the walls drew his attention. He walked over to inspect them. Whatever hardships the sisters had faced, it was obvious they loved each other. In every photo, they were together and smiling or laughing.

He heard the splutter of hot water hitting a coffee mug and glanced back toward the kitchen. Shay stood at the counter, eyes closed as she rubbed the back of her neck and waited for the single-serve machine to finish brewing his cup. An alien sensation traveled through him, starting right in his chest and heading straight to his head. It was a feeling he had never experienced before and one that troubled him.

While he had always enjoyed spoiling the women he kept, he had never in his life been gripped by such an immediate need to protect and pamper one of them. He watched Shay finish his cup of tea and arrange cookies on a plate, all the while picking up on the little signals that told him she was downright exhausted. The desire to draw her a steaming hot bath and bundle her into bed was one that he had to fight.

She's not yours. Drink your tea and go home.

Silently repeating his advice, he shucked his coat, joined her at the round table in the kitchen and spooned some sugar into his tea. "Which university do you attend?"

"U of H," she answered and pushed the plate of cookies toward him. They were delicate snowflakes with white glaze, silver sugar beads and a dusting of blue sprinkles. "I'm studying retailing and consumer sciences."

"You want to run a store someday?" He picked up one of the cookies and took a bite. The slightest hint of citrus from the sugary glaze hit his tongue and offered a decadent after-note to the buttery cookie.

"My goal is to have a brick-and-mortar boutique along with an online storefront to sell the purses and leather goods I design," she explained. "I've got a mentor who has taught me all about leatherwork so I figured that going to college to learn the ins and outs of running a business was a good investment."

"It is. I had to learn the hard way and made quite a few mistakes that first year that really cost me. Luckily, I had friends and acquaintances who were willing to give me advice or send me in the right direction to professionals who could help me." He glanced at the leather purse on the couch. "You made that one?"

"Yes."

"It's very nice. What made you want to design purses?"

"I wanted something pretty but didn't have the money to waste on something so frivolous. You can't eat a purse or pay the light bill with it, you know?" She shrugged. "So I started playing around with fabric and duct tape and empty drink containers. Eventually I figured out I could make a cool looking purse with a hollowed-out book and a wooden handle. There were some girls at school that liked them so I managed to sell a few and make enough money for us to have Christmas that year."

Her entrepreneurial spirit impressed him.

"I started going to that big flea market—"

"The one on Eldridge?"

"Yeah. Have you been there?"

"It's been a while for me."

The massive trading village with thousands of vendors was a place that attracted the best bargain hunters in search of attractively priced new and used merchandise— but also a criminal element that needed to get rid of hot items. He decided not to tell her that he had once been part of a crew that had sold all sorts of cheap, imported and stolen goods there. Bootlegged DVDs had always gone fast. The year Kostya had gotten his hands on a pharmaceutical shipment that had *fallen off* a truck had been a particularly good one…

"Do you still sell there?"

"No. It was good business while I was in high school. Now I have an online store. The overhead is cheaper obviously."

"I would imagine." He finished his tea and eyed the plate of delicious cookies.

"Would you like to take some with you?"

"Do you mind?"

"Of course not." She rose from her chair and fetched a small container from one of the cabinets. "I always bake too much for two people so I'm always handing out containers of cookies or muffins to our neighbors."

"Have you lived here long?"

"Just under three years," she said. "It's not as nice as some of the apartment complexes closer to the university but it's pretty safe and the neighbors are mostly quiet. Plus the rent is cheap."

He bit his tongue instead of offering his opinion. Searching for a safer topic, he thought about her business. "Why did you choose leather?"

"I met Larry at the flea market. He's an old school leather goods guy. Belts, wallets, boots—he's amazing. He let me work in his store and taught me the tricks of the trade."

"Why don't you work there anymore?"

"He closed down. The economy tanked right after he found out he had lung cancer. He beat the hell out of that cancer, but the recession beat the hell out of him. He's retired now and living with his daughter and her family up in the Panhandle. It's better for him there, and he's very happy to be surrounded by his grandkids."

"I'm sure he's happy, but it's damned cold up there."

She laughed. "You're from Russia. It's damned cold

there."

He watched the way she meticulously placed the cookies in the container and separated the layers with strips of wax paper she tore from the roll she had taken out of a nearby drawer. "I've acclimated to the Houston weather. I wouldn't last a day in a Moscow winter."

"Do you think you'll ever go back?"

"No." The answer came swiftly. "That was my old life. This is the new one."

"Just like that, huh?" She pressed the lid onto the container. "You draw that line and close that door and that's that?"

"Yes." He accepted the cookies from her. "It's best not to dwell on things that become tiresome. Cut the problem out of your life and move on."

She studied him for a moment. "And that's your philosophy in life?"

"It's worked well for me." He picked up his cup and carried it to the sink. Cookies in hand, he headed for the door and slipped back into his coat. "Thanks for the tea and the cookies."

"It's the least I could do. You saved me from a run-in with Lalo and got me home safely." Her sensual mouth curved with a playful smile. "It wasn't quite the sleigh ride of Christmas carols, but it'll do."

He laughed. "I'm pretty sure the sleigh from those Christmas carols didn't have heated seats or luxury leather."

"No." She grinned. "The heated seats were a nice touch."

He chose not to make a flirtatious remark about heating up the leather. There was a reason Shay was so tempting to him—and it was because she was different. She deserved so much better than what he had to offer, and he wasn't about to insult her by coming onto her and plying her with gifts and trinkets in exchange for a few hours of affection every week.

"Thank you very much for coming to my rescue tonight."

Coming to her rescue? Jesus, he was nobody's hero!

Still he couldn't stop himself from offering help.

"If you ever need anything, Shay, you come to me first. I'll take care of you—*it*," he hastily amended. "If Lalo's men bother you, I want to know about it. I may not be in that life anymore but I have friends who are."

"Thanks, but I can handle it."

"It's good to be brave, Shay, but it's better to be smart and safe. Let men like me deal with men like Lalo. You're above that and should stay out of it."

Her gaze drifted to the open neck of his shirt where the tops of the onion domed churches inked on his chest were visible. Did she know what they meant? He wanted to know what she was thinking but wasn't courageous enough to ask because he feared the worst.

"All right," she said softly. "I'll come to you if I need help."

"Don't ever hesitate to ask me for anything. My door is always open to you." He shut his mouth before he went too far.

"Thank you. I really appreciate that."

He opened the door and stepped out into the cold, dark night. "Merry Christmas, Shay."

"Merry Christmas…Alexei."

She spoke his name in that gentle voice of hers, and it did crazy things to him. It took every ounce of willpower to drive away from her house. His brain told him to keep his foot on the gas, but the lust and need unfurling within him like a blazing fire urged him to turn around, knock on her door and claim her with a kiss that would leave her breathless and trembling. A few sweet words and promises of money and pretty things would get him through the door and into her bed. That tactic had never failed him.

But he couldn't do that to her.

He *wouldn't* do that to her.

Shay had escaped an entanglement with a dangerous drug dealer tonight. The very last thing she needed was an ex-con and former mobster complicating her life and tarnishing that promising future she was working so hard to build for herself. She was going places, and he refused to be the millstone around that beautiful neck of hers.

As he let himself inside his house and moved through the quiet, empty space, Alexei tried to avoid the painful conclusion about his life that lingered in the far reaches of his brain. Like the house, he was empty inside.

Alone.

After splashing some whisky into a glass, he dropped into his favorite chair and switched on the news. He had just gotten comfortable when his phone started to ring. He glanced at the screen and saw Marissa's smiling face. She was a breathtakingly beautiful woman and looked so utterly tantalizing in that photo, especially with the tanned swell of cleavage peeking over the red fabric of her dress. Any other night, the sight of her photo would have revved his engines and had him thinking about sex—rough, sweaty and hard and exactly the way he liked it.

Now? Well...he felt only irritation. He didn't want another empty encounter. Marissa was a nice woman, and they had had some truly fun times together but she was only in it for the perks. He wasn't innocent in that, of course. His predicament was one of his own making.

Not wanting Marissa stuck inside waiting for him

when she could be out enjoying herself with friends, he sent her a quick text message. *Not tonight.*

She didn't answer.

Tossing aside his phone, he eyed the container of cookies he had placed on the bar. Unable to help himself, he got up to grab them and poured more whisky into his glass. He examined one of the sugary snowflakes and thought of Shay. Beautiful, talented, smart, determined to better herself and a skilled baker? Of course, Shay had to be the whole fucking package.

Loosened up by another two fingers of scotch, he considered asking the janitorial company to take the two sisters off his contract and give him a different cleaning team. Men, he thought sourly. He needed a team of men cleaning his establishment. There would be no temptation that way.

Despite the attractiveness of that solution, he acknowledged it was the wrong one. He simply had to keep his distance. No more late nights when she was due to clean the dealership. If they had to interact, he would keep their conversations short and light.

Thinking of the car he had arranged for Nikolai, he decided that was the template he would follow. He could keep an eye on Shay and make sure she stayed out of trouble. If that sister of hers was intent on hanging with the cartel crowd, Shay would need his help sooner or later. He might not be a hero, but he could step in when necessary to shield and protect her.

Taking another bite of the delicious cookie, he closed his eyes and leaned back in his chair. Shay's smiling face flashed before him. After all the terrible things he had done in his life, maybe Shay was his chance to do something truly good...

Catch up with Alexei and Shay in ALEXEI (Her Russian Protector #8) to be released in Summer 2014!

FROM RUSSIA, WITH LOVE
VASYA

Smile. Laugh. Pretend.

Ty Weston repeated the silent mantra as he mingled with his parents' guests at their annual black tie Christmas Eve gala. The boozy bash was the hottest ticket on Houston's holiday event calendar. It was a who's who of Houston's elite. The old money oil barons, the new gas tycoons from all that fracking going down in the Eagle Ford Shale and the Permian Basin, the athletes, the tech whizzes like Bee Langston, the shipping magnates— everywhere Ty looked he spotted dollar signs.

If it hadn't been for the new crisis PR firm he was starting in the New Year with Lena Cruz, he would have bowed out of this schmooze fest, but it was the cost of doing business. With Lena out of the country on a whirlwind winter vacation with Yuri, that deliciously sexy Russian oligarch she had wrapped around her little finger, the burden of finding clients fell on him.

Despite wanting to be anywhere but here, Ty accepted his duty to their fledgling firm, plastered on a megawatt smile and move around the room. He zeroed in on the group of newly minted gas millionaires because he knew the lot of them were tied up in media scrutiny over fracking practices. Considering his dad came from very old oil money and their wealth was tied up in the energy sector, Ty had all the necessary contacts and knowledge to go after those types of clients.

Though the men welcomed him warmly, he had long ago learned to spot the ones who were uneasy around a gay man. The tightness in the jaw, the smile that never quite reached the eyes, the stiff laughter—he mentally checked the boxes as he chatted with the group. Of the five men, two would never be clients and he crossed them off his list. The other three seemed receptive so he made sure to hand out his business cards and encouraged them to stop by the new offices or drop him a line via email.

On the prowl for his next mark, Ty spotted his baby sister Caitlin stuck in a corner with the football player their mother had arranged as a date. Poor Cait had that nervous smile on her face, the one that told him that she was about to have a freaking panic attack. Her sensitive ears hated loud music like this, and she struggled so badly in social situations. The protective streak within him ignited. Wanting to save her from yet another terrible setup, he weaved his way through the crowd.

"Don't even think about it, Tyrone." His mother's hissed voice dinged his ear as her icy hand gripped his wrist.

He closed his eyes and clenched his teeth rather than shake off her hold. Fully aware they were surrounded by the eyes and ears of the society press, he affected a smile and embraced his mother in a way that seemed loving. Sliding his arm around her shoulders, he murmured, "She's miserable. She needs to be rescued."

"She's never going to learn how to be normal if you're always running interference for her."

His lips twitched as he smothered a snarled reply. Normal? What the fuck was normal anyway? "She's doing the best she can."

"She could do better."

Deftly untangling himself from the woman who had given birth to him but who had shown him so little love, he ignored her order and continued his trek across the hotel ballroom. Issuing commands might work in D.C. where his mother was one of the most powerful U.S. senators, but it didn't fly here. Her power over him had ended many years ago. Now if he could only free Cait...

"Sugar," he swept in and pecked her cheek. "I don't think I've met your friend." He knew the football player by sight and reputation but wanted to be polite.

"His name is Quade Dykstra." She relaxed into his brotherly hug. "He's a line receiver on the football team."

Quade frowned. "Wide receiver."

"Oh. Right." She looked mortified at her gaffe. "He's a wide receiver."

"It's nice to meet you, Quade." To his credit, Quade didn't hesitate to shake hands with him. Considering the photographers milling around the place, it said a lot about the football player to know that he wasn't reticent about being photographed getting chummy with an openly gay man.

"Nice to meet you, too."

"So what have you two been chatting about all night?"

"Your sister was telling me all about her telescopes and the research she's been doing at Rice for the last three years."

Ty inwardly winced. Once Cait started talking about her work, she had such a hard time turning off the spout of knowledge that wanted to keep pouring from her mouth. Smiling at Quade, he playfully asked, "Did we learn anything interesting?"

"She told about that asteroid she discovered."

"Comet," Ty corrected carefully. "She discovered a comet."

"Right," Quade said with embarrassment. He glanced at Cait. "Sorry."

"It's fine." Her clipped reply convinced Ty she was anything but fine.

An uncomfortably tight silence settled around their trio. Ty wasn't at all surprised when Quade's gaze flicked to a small group of nearby women. Wanting to make the transition easy for everyone, he tapped Quade's arm and said, "Well, I hope you don't mind but I need to borrow my sister for the rest of the night. Is that okay?"

"Oh. Um…sure." Quade couldn't hide the relief on his handsome, clean-cut face. The popular athlete bent down to give Cait a quick hug and smiled down at her. "I had a nice time, Caitlin."

"As did I." She parroted the expected reply, but Ty sensed she hadn't enjoyed herself at all.

The football player didn't ask to see her again or stick around a moment longer than necessary. He had the decency to head for the bar instead of making a beeline to the bevy of big-haired Texas beauties who wanted a chance to roll around in his bed.

"I really screwed that one up, didn't I?" Caitlin sounded so down on herself, and it just killed him. "I tried, but I was so worried about what to say and what *not* to say and then he asked about work and I thought maybe he really was interested so I—"

"Sugar," he interrupted gently with a finger to her lips. "Breathe. In. Out." She followed his directions to the letter, and he lowered his hand. "Did you like him?"

"He was okay."

"Just okay?" There were women who would sell an ovary for a chance to date Quade, but Cait seemed totally oblivious to his charms.

"He had a nice smile. He was kind to me."

"A nice smile and kindness is a good place to start."

"I don't think I'll see him again." Her eyes were trained on the bar where Quade chatted up a stunning brunette.

"No, I don't think you will." Cait had always preferred honesty so he gave it to her in black and white. "Look, not every date is going to work out, okay? There will be some really fantastic dates and some truly awkward ones."

"Some of them are fantastic?" She looked skeptical. "All of my dates are awkward." Her mouth slanted. "This is pointless. I keep asking Mom not to make me do these but—"

"Stop asking her, Caitlin. Just tell her." He placed his hand against her cheek. "Sweetheart, you're twenty-three years old. You're a world-renowned astronomer. I've watched you stand up to Nobel Prize winning scientists to prove your theories. You can stand up to our mother."

"And then what?" she asked nervously. "What happens after I tell her no more interfering?"

"You date the guys you want to date." He considered the way her Asperger's Syndrome affected her life. The same differences in her brain that made her a brilliant scientist also caused her such difficulties in her personal life. Her very mild form of autism made it difficult for her to understand the social norms that he took for granted. She never let it stop her from trying new things though. Sometimes he stood in awe of the courage she displayed. "Or you don't date at all. It's up to *you*. Whatever you want to do is okay, Cait."

"I do want to date. I want to fall in love and be happy."

"But?"

"But I can't even get a date unless my mom sets me up!"

"You can get a date. You're just not looking in the right places."

Perplexed, she asked, "What are the right places?"

"There's not a master list, Cait. You have to go out and have fun for yourself. The right guy will eventually cross your path. Sort of like that comet of yours," he added with a wink.

That didn't cheer her up. In fact, it seemed to make her even more panicked. "Oh God, Ty! Do you know what the statistical probability of me finding that comet was? If you consider the number of single men of marriageable age and the various places I visit in, say, a one year period and then factor in—"

"Cait," he interjected with a laugh. "Honey, you're doing it again."

She rolled her lips under. "Sorry."

"It's okay. We'll work on it, okay?" He linked their arms together and pecked her cheek. "After the New Year, we'll practice. I'll hold a boot camp at my place, and I'll teach you the art of dating."

"You make it sound so easy."

"You mastered calculus in, like, kindergarten, Cait. You can learn the rules of dating in no time."

"And then?"

"And then I'll unleash you on Houston's single men," he said with a laugh and twirled her onto the dance floor.

Smiling, she let him tug her close and lead her in the two-step. "What about you, Ty? Do you think you'll find the one?"

She had that unnerving way of always asking the one question he didn't want to answer. Tonight was no exception. "I've got my eyes open. If he crosses my path, I'll snatch him right up."

He didn't tell her about the big sexy beast of a Russian who had crossed his path a few months earlier. Dark-haired and handsome, Vasya Fedorov made Ty's heart race and his palms sweat. He hadn't felt so excited or nervous around a man since the first time he had recognized his attraction to Jeb that summer at the country club. What a lifetime ago that was!

Lena's new Russian bodyguard had him all torn up inside, never knowing if he was coming or going. He had been sure at Benny Burkhart and Dimitri Stepanov's wedding that he was going to finally get Vasya right where he wanted him. The silent, brooding Russian had beckoned him to follow, and Ty had bounded after him like a puppy chasing its new master.

But once Vasya had him alone in that cabin on Yuri's yacht, the burly man had shut him down. Ty hadn't even been able to sneak a kiss. Vasya had accused him of being too much of a player to date. Apparently the slightly older man didn't do one-night stands or casual hookups. To say Ty had been shocked was an understatement. Even now, nearly three weeks later, he didn't know how to process that bizarre interaction.

"I've been invited to visit Moscow."

"What?" He missed a step but managed to recover quickly. Pulling back slightly, he peered into his sister's face. "When?"

"February. The ISON network is headquartered there."

She said it as if he should know what that meant. "And that's important because?"

"Because they have dozens of telescopes and data crunching centers solely focused on tracking objects in space," she explained.

"Like your comet?"

She smiled. "Like my comet."

"Well—then you have to go, right?"

"I think I do."

"Do you *want* to go?"

She shrugged. "I speak Russian fluently so that's not an issue. I don't enjoy the physical act of traveling but I do enjoy new places. I would like to be face-to-face with some of the colleagues I've been corresponding with via email for the last few months."

"I think you should go, Caitlin. It will be good for your career. How long will you stay?"

"A university there has offered to host me through the summer. The department here supports the exchange." She glanced around and lowered her voice. "I haven't spoken to mom yet. Dad said he was thrilled when I spoke to him earlier this morning."

"I'm sure he's very proud of you, Cait." Ty scanned the room for their father, not at all surprised to find the man on the complete opposite side of the ballroom from their mother and chatting up a woman who couldn't be any older than Cait.

Why their parents had remained in a marriage that made them both miserable confounded Ty. Divorce wasn't nearly the coffin nail that it had once been for politicians, and their father had made sure to get a pre-nup before tying the knot so money wasn't the issue. Obviously, something held them together, but he had never been able to figure out what the hell it was.

"Will you come see me in Russia?"

"Of course!"

"Promise?"

"Yes." So happy for Cait's skyrocketing career, he kissed her cheek and continued to spin her around the dance floor. He took care to keep her on the far side, away from the live band. Though sensitive to loud noises, she took great pains to attempt to function like a neurotypical. Learning to dance and going out with her tight-knit group of friends was one way she had attempted to tackle her fear of social situations. She might struggle with subtle emotional cues, but she had quickly mastered the art of dance and seemed to love the constant motion.

Just after nine, he sneaked her off the dance floor and out to the lobby where they handed over their valet tickets. With the family photographs out of the way earlier in the evening, there was no reason for them to stick around any longer. They had done their duty to their mother by posing in her holiday snapshots and faking the perfect happy family. Their part played, it was time to bail.

"Would you like to come over for breakfast?" he asked as she slid behind the wheel of her coupe. "I'll make pancakes."

"Okay. I'd like that."

"Great. Um—let's say nine or nine-thirty?"

She blinked twice. "Which one, Ty? You have to pick."

Rolling his eyes, he gave one of her long blonde curls a playful tug. "Nine-thirty."

"All right. I'll be there at nine-thirty. Should I bring something?"

"Just your smile, sweetness." He gave her one last goodnight smooch before shutting her door and walking back to his idling car. The drive to the penthouse he had purchased earlier that year in the Museum District wasn't very far. Too tired to deal with the parking garage, he pulled into the curved drive and chose to use the valet. He pressed a nice tip into Tony's hand because it was so cold out and headed into the building.

The concierge smiled at him as he neared the main desk. "Good evening, Mr. Weston. How was the gala?"

"It was nice. Do I have any mail, Joel?"

"Yes, sir." Joel grabbed the letters from his slot and passed them over. "Here you are, Mr. Weston."

He glanced at the addresses. "My sister will be stopping by in the morning. You know how she can be about showing up too early."

Joel chuckled knowingly. "I'll make sure Casey knows to gently prod her into the elevator so she isn't waiting down here for half an hour again."

"Thank you."

"It's my pleasure." Joel pointed to the seating area in the lobby. "There's a gentleman waiting to see you, Mr. Weston. He said he's a friend but he wasn't on the guest list. I thought he might be a colleague of Mr. Novakovsky's so I had a pot of tea sent out to him while he waited for you."

"A friend of Yuri's?"

"He's Russian. I just assumed."

"Thanks." Ty tapped his mail on the concierge desk and backed away to see this mysterious visitor. He had taken exactly three steps into the main area of the lobby before his heart stuttered in his chest and the breath rushed from his lungs. "Vasya?"

The giant Russian rose from the leather sectional where he had been reading a magazine. He made a simple V-neck tee and blazer paired with jeans look insanely sexy. "Good evening, Ty."

"Um...hi." At a loss for words, Ty stared at the man

who had the starring role in his dreams. "I thought you were in Russia with Yuri and Lena."

"I was."

"But?"

"But I decided it was time for me to take a vacation."

"To Houston?"

"It is where you are—and that is where I want to be."

Mouth dry, Ty wondered at Vasya's change of heart. "Why?"

Glancing around, Vasya asked, "Can we speak somewhere more private?"

"Sure." Ty decided he really wanted to hear whatever Vasya had to say. "You can come up to my place."

"I would like that." Vasya bent down and retrieved a red gift box adorned with gold ribbon that had been hidden from Ty's view.

"It's this way." Trying not to get too excited about the gift Vasya held, Ty led the Russian hunk to the elevators and retrieved his keycard to activate the private access to his penthouse suite.

The doors had barely closed before Vasya reached out and traced the lapel of his tuxedo. "You look very nice tonight."

"If I had known you were going to be in town, I would have made sure you had a ticket to the gala."

"That is not my crowd."

Enclosed in the small space with Vaysa, Ty grew intensely aware of the bigger man's body heat and the intoxicating scent that emanated from him. He wanted to slide closer and bury his nose against the curve of Vasya's neck to inhale that deliciously masculine smell, a mixture of leather and spice that drove him crazy.

"It could be your crowd." He instantly hated the neediness that filled his voice. "If you wanted it to be."

Vasya's thumb drew a lazy circle on his neck. "Let's talk first."

Talk? Ty had hoped for a little more than talking but he would take what he could get from Vasya, especially if there was a promise of something more. The man had shown up at his building and waited for him. Surely that meant Vasya was having second thoughts about rejecting his advances on the yacht.

Once inside his penthouse, Ty shrugged out of his tuxedo jacket. "Would you like something to drink? A glass of wine? A beer? Coffee?"

"I'm not staying that long."

Disappointment arced through him. "No?"

"No." Vasya approached him, stopping so close they were breathing each other's air, and presented him with the gift. "Merry Christmas, Tyrone."

He accepted the box and smiled up at Vasya. "Thank you—but I can't take this."

The Russian's jaw hardened. "Why not?"

Ty touched Vasya's strong forearm and marveled at the hard muscle beneath his fingertips. "Because I didn't get you anything," he admitted, feeling suddenly bashful.

"Oh." Vasya shrugged those broad shoulders. "It's not my Christmas yet. You have plenty of time to return the favor."

Not his Christmas yet? It dawned on him that Vasya meant the Orthodox celebration that occurred in early January. "Well…okay. If I still have time to shop for you, I can take your gift."

Vasya's massive hand settled over his, preventing Ty from opening the box. "Wait until I'm gone."

Surprised by the instruction, he glanced up into the Russian's pale blue eyes. Mesmerized by the icy shade, he nodded. "Are you sure you don't want to stay for a drink?"

Or the night…

"I shouldn't."

"Why not?"

"Because we're going to do things differently," Vasya stated matter-of-factly.

"How so?"

Vasya dragged his thick finger along Ty's jaw and brushed it across his lower lip. "How long was your last relationship?"

"Relationship? I don't really do those." He squirmed under Vasya's intense scrutiny. "I had a boyfriend I loved when I was in high school but that started and ended during a summer."

"So three months?"

He gulped nervously. "About."

"I want more than three months."

"Do you?" He shivered inside as Vasya's smoldering gaze swept him.

"Yes." The Russian tapped the tip of his nose. "I think that's the way you protect yourself. You jump in and out of bed and rush things before they have time to develop."

"Do I?" In the back of his mind, Ty thought he should probably be pissed off at Vasya for insinuating that he was so promiscuous, but there was just something so calming about the way the bigger man cupped the back of his neck and brushed his fingertips up and down his skin.

"I've watched you for months. I refuse to be one of those men you fuck and abandon. We're not going to do things your way."

Ty swallowed hard. "We're not?"

"*Nyet*. We do this my way—or we don't do it all."

"I really, *really* want to do it your way."

Vasya grinned. "Patience."

He rolled his eyes at the mistaken double entendre and playfully pinched Vasya's arm. "I meant dating."

"Are you sure?" The Russian looked dead serious. "I warn you now, Ty. I'm not playing around with you. If you say that you are mine, then you are mine. Understand?"

"Oh, yes." He toyed with one of the buttons on Vasya's blazer. "So—how does your way work?"

"First, you put my name on your list of approved guests. I'm not waiting in your lobby anymore."

"Okay," he agreed excitedly. Vasya's aggressive manner sparked something primal within Ty.

"Then I pick you up tomorrow and we have dinner."

"And then?"

"And then I bring you home."

"Home?" He deflated a little. "That's it? Do I get a good night kiss at least?"

The corners of Vasya's mouth lifted with amusement. "At the very least," he promised.

Ty thought that sounded better. "Okay. Dinner and a good night kiss is good. Actually, it sounds like an old-fashioned romance."

Vasya broke into a full grin now. "Well, baby, it won't be *that* old-fashioned."

The endearment washed over him like sunshine. "No, I suppose not."

With a couple of well-placed steps, Vasya backed him up against the nearest wall. An average-sized man with a lean swimmer's build, Ty didn't often feel small, but boxed in by that hard, wide chest, he had nowhere to look but straight up at the giant who towered over him. Heart racing and lightheaded, he watched the slow descent of Vasya's mouth. He couldn't remember feeling this excited since his first kiss.

Except there was nothing fumbling or uncertain about Vasya's technique. He was all man, all brawn and so impossibly powerful. He kissed like a master, his skilled tongue darting between Ty's lips to taste him. Gripping Vasya's arm, Ty surrendered to this alpha male who seemed intent on capturing and keeping him forever. Right now, Ty couldn't imagine anything better.

When their feverish kiss finally ended, they were both breathing hard. Vasya placed a gentle, tender kiss to Ty's forehead before straightening up. "I'll pick you up at eight tomorrow."

"Okay." His tingling lips were barely able to form that one word.

"Good night, Ty."

"Good night, Vasya."

Leaning against the wall for support, Ty watched the Russian stud leave his apartment. Butterflies went wild in his belly as he let himself dream of building something *real* with the mysterious and complicated man. The idea of an old-fashioned romance, one where Vasya treated him like something precious and respected him, sounded so very good.

Carrying the box to the couch, he sank down onto the cushion to save his shaky legs and carefully untied the ribbons. He lifted the lid—and laughed out loud. Inside the box sat a traditionally decorated *matryoshka*. Amused by Vasya's sense of humor, he turned the nesting doll over in his hand to examine it.

Wondering if there was anything inside, Ty carefully separated the two halves and discovered a smaller doll. He separated that one and was rewarded by a small package wrapped in white tissue paper. Setting aside the doll, he tore open the tissue paper and discovered an exquisitely handcrafted leather bracelet. He ran his fingers over the braided strips and along the sterling silver tag dangling like a charm.

Bringing the small tag closer to his eyes, he read the two initials inscribed on one side—V and T—and the message on the other one. *From Russia, With Love.*

Exhaling happily, Ty slid on the bracelet and dropped back against the couch. There was no stopping the giddiness that bubbled out of him and made him grin. He didn't know where this thing with Vasya was going but he couldn't wait to get started!

Catch up with Ty and Vasya in a full-length novel to be released in Fall 2014!

ALL I WANT FOR CHRISTMAS
NIKOLAI

Sticking to the shadows of his restaurant, mob boss and restaurateur Nikolai Kalasnikov leaned his shoulder against the wall and watched his staff cutting loose and enjoying a well-earned night of carefree partying. As hard as they worked during the year, they all deserved to eat good food, enjoy the open bar and dance until they dropped. Two and a half hours into the party, some of them looked like they were just about to reach that point. Whether it was the free-flowing cocktails or the lateness of the evening, he couldn't tell.

His amused gaze turned heated as it fell upon Vivian Valero. With her head thrown back in laughter, she presented such a tantalizing vision. The emerald shade of the lacy dress she wore complemented her black hair and bright blue eyes to utter perfection. He instantly recognized the diamond bracelet adorning her wrist as the one he had given her last Christmas. They matched the earrings dangling from her ears, the same set he had gifted her on her birthday.

As if she sensed him watching her, Vee glanced away from the small group she chatted with and smiled at him. Bewitched by her beautiful face, he returned her friendly look. One mischievous little wink from her and his heart raced. The cherry red hue on her lips tempted him greatly. If he kissed her, how would she taste? Sweet, he surmised. Intoxicating.

Refusing to surrender to the dangerous yearning he felt toward the young woman he guarded from afar, he broke their shared gaze. Their friendship was complicated enough without him looking at her like a lovesick puppy.

Nikolai spotted one of his enforcers lumbering through the kitchen entrance. He checked the black leather stretched across Sergei's broad shoulders for any signs of precipitation but saw nothing. He hoped the wintry mix of rain and sleet had finally stopped for the night. He wanted everything to go perfectly tonight—and bad weather wasn't part of those plans.

Without having to be beckoned, Sergei knew he was needed. The great big bear of a man edged the dance floor where couples were laughing and swinging their hips. The enforcer's hawk-like gaze swept the restaurant even as he delivered his update. "Everything is arranged in the garage, and the drivers have already started lining up out back. Bobby wanted me to tell you that he sent over extra taxis, just in case."

Arranging rides to and from the Christmas party was another way he took care of his people. Quite a few of the kitchen staff relied on public transportation. Those who had their own vehicles often chose the free rides so they could indulge in the open bar without worrying about how they would get home.

"Good." He clapped Sergei's back. "I'll be in the office

getting the bonuses ready. Ask the DJ to start winding down the night."

"Done."

Moving into the rear offices of Samovar, Nikolai unlocked his office door. He punched in the code for the safe and withdrew the sack of envelopes holding the holiday bonuses he gave to every employee. He based them on the years they had been at his restaurant, making sure to give extra to the workers who had busted their asses the most, gotten the highest reviews from customers and to the ones who were having difficulties at home.

The bonuses in hand, he returned to the restaurant's main floor. He took a moment to enjoy the view of the festively decorated space. Despite all that he had accomplished in life and as high as he had climbed, he still had moments where he was taken aback by his successes. While he would like nothing more than to shake off the stain of his involvement in Maksim Prokhorov's crime family, Nikolai understood that was a dream. He was in too deep—and there was no escape.

Here, in the real world, he had managed a rare feat. He kept one foot in Houston's underworld and one in the light of day where he was acknowledged as a successful businessman—and whispered about as perhaps something a bit more. It was a delicate balance but one Nikolai had maintained so far.

Blending into the crowd of Samovar employees and their dates were the men who formed his Houston branch of the crime family. Some of his captains—Artyom, Ilya and Evgeni—had attended with their close-knit crews. Nikolai's own hand-picked men—Sergei, Danila, and Kostya—were constantly moving inside and outside of the restaurant, keeping an eye on things and making sure that nothing spoiled the night.

A flutter of green lace caught his eye. One of the kitchen boys spun Vivian around the dance floor and held her entirely too close for Nikolai's liking. Dark-haired and dashing, Aaron was a medical student who picked up extra hours at the restaurant whenever possible. Lately, Aaron seemed to be putting his name on the schedule only when Vivian was waitressing. It was a coincidence that hadn't escaped Nikolai's notice.

Hating the streak of jealousy that blazed through him, Nikolai clenched the stack of bonuses. He wanted to be the one gliding Vee around the dance floor. He wanted to be the one making her laugh and smile and the one she playfully kissed under that spring of mistletoe. All he wanted for Christmas was Vivian.

Inhaling a slow breath, he silently listed all the reasons he couldn't claim her as his woman. His entanglement with Houston's criminal underbelly ranked top of the list. His history with her incarcerated father, a notorious enforcer for an outlaw motorcycle club tied in with the Guzman cartel out of Mexico, was a close second.

And then, of course, there was the secret he had been keeping from her for more than a decade. A secret that would kill their friendship and send her fleeing from him forever…

Young and innocent, she was a wildly talented artist with the whole wide world ahead of her. He couldn't have what he so desperately wanted with her but he could protect and support her. Anything she wanted or needed was hers. She didn't even have to ask. He prided himself on anticipating her needs and fulfilling them before she had a chance to seek his help. Despite knowing what was best for her, Nikolai couldn't stop the painful ache that twisted his heart anytime she was near. Like now…

"You're not dancing!" A bit breathless with cheeks flushed from laughter, she came to stand in front of him. "The party is almost over. If you're going to dance—"

"I don't dance, Vee." He inhaled that soft lavender scent that followed her everywhere.

Her smile faded and her expression grew concerned. Unlike everyone else, she didn't fear him enough to keep her hands to herself. She reached out and placed a gentle hand on his forearm. "You know it's all right to let yourself have fun every now and then. You don't always have to wear the mask. You can just be *you*, Kolya."

The searing heat of her touch burned right through the sleeve of his suit jacket. His gaze settled on those pouty lips that had just issued a nickname only she dared to use in public. Outside his closest friends only Vivian had earned the right to speak to him with such friendliness and ease.

His fingers itched to reach out and stroke the silky waves of black hair that curled around her shoulders. He shut down the need to touch her and ignored the pulsing ache in his chest. "I'm the boss. It's not appropriate for me to dance with the employees."

"Which boss is that?" Those pretty blue eyes of hers were now framed by arched eyebrows. She had nailed him with that question. "Are you the boss of Samovar tonight? Or are you the boss of—"

"Vee," he cut her off with a stern look. "Don't."

Her face fell. "I'm sorry, Mr. Kalasnikov. I won't forget my place again."

Shit. "Vee—"

But she had already spun on her heel. He took a step toward her but squashed the urge to follow her and make it right. She was his weakness, and one he simply shouldn't indulge. Yet even as he moved onto the dance floor to give his usual speech and start the process of handing out bonuses, Nikolai understood it was impossible.

As he let his employees know how much he appreciated their hard work and the way they continually upheld the sterling reputation of restaurant, he tried not to be aware of Vivian standing just outside his line of sight. She stood between Aaron and the sous-chef Oleg who had long had a crush on her. No doubt his curtness toward her had put her in a mindset that was favorable toward either man. Would this be the night he lost her to a worthier man without a dark past and a soul stained by sin?

While he handed out bonuses to the line of employees queuing up to meet him, the catering staff he had hired for the night started to clear away the tables and tidy up the restaurant. The line grew shorter and shorter, but Vivian was nowhere to be seen. Aaron and Oleg were among the last to shake his hand. When Oleg grasped the envelope extended toward him, Nikolai held onto it. "Where is Vivian?"

The sous-chef glanced around and finally spotted her. "Over there. She's making sure everyone donated to Manuel's jar."

"Jar?" He craned his neck for a better look at her. She grasped a large jar decorated in holiday colors and wheedled donations out of everyone heading out the door.

"Should I take her home?"

Nikolai pinned Oleg with a cold stare. "No."

The incredibly skilled cook inclined his head with respect. "Okay, boss."

After Oleg moved along, he finished handing out the remaining bonuses and stopped to speak with the general manager. Certain the restaurant was in good hands, Nikolai sought out Vivian who was making the rounds of his men and persuading them to open their wallets with that sweet smile of hers. When she whirled around after getting Kostya to donate a few crisp twenties, she knocked into Nikolai's chest. He steadied her and was glad for the plastic jar wedged between their bodies.

"Oh! Sorry."

"Be careful, Vee. In those heels, you're easily knocked off balance."

"Don't I know it," she said with a laugh. "I nearly ate it three times on the dance floor tonight!"

He let his hands drop from her upper arms and took the jar from her. She had taped heart wrenching photos of Manuel, his wife Maria and the two premature twins she had delivered three weeks earlier. Last week, they had lost one of the twins—a baby girl—to complications from being so severely premature. Their son remained in the NICU of the world-class children's hospital downtown. Nikolai hoped for the best but he wasn't optimistic.

"For the expenses from the funeral and living costs," she said sadly. "I know it would help them if they could replace Maria's income so she can stay at the hospital with their baby."

Her soft heart touched him and the kind gesture toward her friend and fellow employee filled him with pride. "I've made arrangements to help them. It's not nearly enough. Money will never bring back their baby, but it's all I can do."

She smiled at him. "I knew you would do something to help."

Her unshakeable belief in his ability to be good unsettled him. Most people assumed the worst of him but not Vivian. She seemed to always see the best. "Do you want me to lock that in my office?"

"Would you mind? I planned to give it to him on the weekend when he comes in to work."

"I don't mind." He backed away from her and gave one final order. "Get your coat and wait for me. I'll take you home."

After locking the jar in the safe, Nikolai made a final round of the restaurant, gave Sergei and Danny the night off and found Kostya lingering near the rear exit with an armload of gifts. Vivian stood nearby with Igor, the elderly host who welcomed guests to the restaurant and handled all of the hospitality. These cold evenings were hard on Igor's arthritic hands so she helped button the front of his coat and curled his scarf around his neck, giving it an artful knot. The older man sweetly pecked her cheeks before bidding her farewell.

Eyeing Kostya's armload, Nikolai teasingly asked, "Secret admirers?"

Kostya shot him a look. "Not mine, boss."

Grabbing the nearest tag, he read the names there and scowled. It seemed the Secret Santa rules that the employees used to keep costs down had been scuttled for Vivian. There were at least a dozen small boxes and gift bags with her name on them, all of them given by men who worked at the restaurant. Irritated by the way other men dared to shower *his* Vee with gifts, Nikolai was ready to start writing out pink slips.

But she's not my Vee.

For now, she belonged to no man, but how long would that last? She already had some sort of relationship brewing with that bodyguard Kelly Connolly. He had seen them together at Dimitri and Benny's wedding. There might not be romantic feelings between them yet, but it seemed a likely outcome. One thing Nikolai knew for sure. He could never compete with a man like Kelly. The former Marine was a true war hero with a stand-up reputation.

If it wasn't Kelly who stole her away from the protective bubble he had placed around her, it would be someone else. She was starting to make forays into the art scene in Houston and rubbing shoulders with wealthy patrons from all around the world. How long before one of them noticed the same qualities he did and decided to make a move on her?

There was so much he couldn't offer Vivian that other men—better men—could. Wasn't it best for her to find a man that could make her proud? A man who lived his life totally in the light of day? Wasn't that what he had always wanted for her? To escape the hell she had known when she had been all tangled up in her father's crimes and orphaned by her sick mother?

He wanted Vivian to have a good life. That meant he had to accept that his complex feelings toward her—the love he dared not confess—would remain forever a secret. She would marry, have children and embark on a journey filled with laughter and light and love.

And he would stay in this dark underworld, running Houston's criminal element and keeping the lid on the violence that always threatened to erupt. He would die alone, without a wife, without children—and he would be forgotten.

"Are you all right?" Vivian stood in front of him now and gazed up at him with such concern. "You look so sad."

He flashed her an empty smile. "It's nothing. Let's get you home."

She looked like she wanted to press him on the issue,

but thankfully she let it drop. He took the coat from her arms, shook it out and helped her into it. While she buttoned the front, he grasped the silky strands of her loose hair and gently pulled them free from the back of her coat. The tantalizing lavender fragrance of her shampoo and the light scent of her perfume sorely tried his control.

Dropping his hands to his sides, he waited for her to slip into her gloves before escorting her outside to the idling SUV where Kostya loaded her gifts into the cargo area. He helped her into a seat and moved to the front passenger side. "Do you need to make any stops tonight?"

"No."

"Well I need to make one so you'll have to bear with me." He hoped she would like the gift he had picked out for her.

"That's fine."

Kostya got behind the wheel and made a stealthy adjustment of the weapon he carried everywhere. As Nikolai's right hand man and the family cleaner, Kostya was always prepared for the very worst. It had been a calm year around Houston's underbelly, all things considered, but the seedy world they inhabited had a way of turning violent in a flash.

The drive to the nearby parking garage he owned was quick enough. The roads were wet but not icy as he had feared. After her old car had died last year, Vivian had chosen to use public transportation. She was too much out of practice for wintry conditions, but a little rain, he thought she could handle.

Round and round, they climbed the levels of the garage until they reached the last covered floor. Only half the spaces were filled and the far wall was entirely open except for the brand new sporty luxury coupe topped with a bright red bow. In the backseat, Vivian had her head down as she messed around with her phone and seemed totally oblivious to the surprise that awaited her as Kostya pulled into a space.

Glancing at Kostya, Nikolai climbed out of the vehicle. He walked around the back of the SUV and opened her door. Vivian looked perplexed. "Kolya?"

"I want to show you something."

She frowned. "In a parking lot?"

With the SUV facing away from the car, she couldn't see it. Amused by her reaction, he held out his hand. "Humor me, Vee."

"All right." She placed her gloved hand on his, the leather cool against his skin, and slipped out of the backseat to join him.

"Grab your purse." She would need her wallet while she drove. Shooting him an odd look, she did as instructed. He walked her toward the back of the SUV and knew the moment she spotted the new car.

A gasp escaped her lips. "Nikolai!"

Grinning, he dug the keys out of his pocket and turned to hand them over to her. "*S Rozhdestvom.* Merry Christmas, Vee."

Her pink lips remained parted with shock. She blinked a few times and glanced from the keyless fob resting on his outstretched hand to the vehicle adorned with a bow and then his face. "But—we never exchange gifts until January."

They had always waited for the traditional Orthodox Christmas date to trade gifts, but this year he had decided to give her the car a few days early. "I wanted you to have it now."

"A car?" She looked troubled and bit her lower lip with indecision. "Did you get this from Alexei Sarnov?"

"Yes. He helped me pick it out."

She wrung her hands. "But it's so expensive."

"It's a gift, Vivian. The price doesn't matter." He placed the key onto her hand and curled her gloved fingers around it. "You're worth it to me."

Her gaze skipped to his face. Eyes wide, she stared up at him with an expression he couldn't place. For a moment, he thought that maybe, just maybe, she felt the same stirrings of love and desire that he experienced every time she was near, but he shoved aside those fanciful thoughts. She saw him as her protector and nothing more. That was the way it had to be.

"I swore that I would look out for you. Before they died, I promised your grandparents that you would be taken care of and get a good start in the world. This is my way of holding up that promise."

A fleeting glint of sadness darkened her eyes. He silently cursed himself for bringing up the only family who had ever shown her kindness or love. The holidays were hard enough for her without being forced to think of the two people she had lost too soon.

"So that's it?" she asked carefully. "This is just your way of keeping a promise?"

Now it was his turn to frown at her. "Of course. What else could it possibly be?"

Had she figured out that his feelings toward her weren't completely platonic? Did it frighten her to think of him that way? Was she worried he would try to force her to become his woman?

"I see."

He couldn't read her voice or her face. Something had just happened between them and damned if he knew what it meant or what he had gotten wrong. Somewhere along the way, their wires had crossed, and now he was the one on the receiving end of a painful jolt.

"Come on." He motioned toward the car. "You can drive me to your apartment. Kostya will follow us."

She hesitated before trailing him to the car. Her gloved hand glided over the sleek lines of the luxury coupe and patted the showy bow. Studying the key fob, she found the unlock button and pressed it. Nikolai took care of the bow and stowed it in the backseat before sliding into the passenger seat next to her. She figured out how to use the push button start and then stared at the touchscreen that operated the radio, navigational program and more.

"I don't know how to use this."

He wasn't surprised. Her last vehicle had been thirteen or fourteen years old. The CD player had been the most technologically advanced item in it. "Here. I'll show you."

Because he had a similar vehicle in his collection, Nikolai was familiar with the interface. He showed her how easy it was to work the climate control and laughed at the scandalized look that crossed her face when he activated her seat warmer. When she handed over her MP3 player, he synced it up with the stereo so she could listen to her music while she drove.

"If I catch you texting or talking while you drive, I will be extremely disappointed, Vee." He held her gaze a moment before establishing the Bluetooth connection between her phone and the car. "Promise me that you will be safe."

"I promise I'll be safe if I drive."

"If?" He seized on the word as he dropped her phone into a cup holder. "What do you mean *if?*"

She traced the stitching along the curve of the steering wheel. "I don't think I can accept this car, Nikolai. It's…too much." She fingered the diamond bracelet he had given her last year. "This was borderline, but I accepted it because I saw happy it made you to give it to me. This car?" She ran her hand along the dash. "It's just way, way overboard for a gift between friends."

Between friends. The words shouldn't have gutted him but they did.

"I want you to have it, Vee." He slashed his hand through the air. "This isn't up for discussion. You're keeping it."

She stared at him for an unnervingly long moment. "I'm not a member of your crew, Nikolai. You don't get to use that tone with me."

Remembering the way he had hurt her feelings back at the party, he sought to make things right. "I shouldn't have been so short with you when you needled me about which boss I was tonight. That was wrong of me, and I'm sorry if it hurt you."

"You did, but I know I crossed a line. Sometimes I forget that our friendship has rules." She shrugged, as if nervous, and admitted, "I don't always know what we are or what we're doing."

He didn't either. The last few weeks, especially, he seemed to be skating dangerously close to *that* line with her. "We're friends. I'm your protector. I'm the man you come to when you have a problem that needs solving."

"Is that all you are to me?" She asked the question as if she didn't know the answer.

God, how he wanted to be more. He wanted to be *everything* to her. "It's all I can be, Vivian."

She studied his face and then exhaled slowly. "Okay."

"You'll keep the car?"

She picked up her MP3 player and chose a Christmas playlist. "No."

"Vee—"

"This car costs, like, five times what I earn in a year

between working at the restaurant and selling some of my paintings. It is way, way beyond my means to keep it insured and do the required maintenance. It's beautiful, Nikolai, but it's not the car for me."

Recognizing that stubborn streak, he decided to table the discussion for tonight. He had absolutely zero intention of letting her give the car back. If she refused to keep the keys, he would leave it parked in front of her apartment building until she changed her mind. Two could play this game—and he would win.

"The car has a service package. You just take it to Alexei Sarnov's dealership, and they'll handle everything. I've already arranged your insurance policy." She narrowed her eyes at him, and he held up his hands. "All right. I'll stop."

Despite her protestations about keeping the vehicle, it was clear that she loved driving it as she carefully navigated the wet streets and the surprisingly empty interstate. When they reached her apartment complex, she parked carefully and seemed almost reluctant to shut down the engine. He wanted to ask her if she had changed her mind but let the question die on his tongue.

"Come inside with me. I'll give you your gift since we're breaking tradition this year."

"All right." Kostya had pulled into a nearby space so he slid out of the front seat, ambled over to the SUV and retrieved all the gifts Vivian's admirers had given her at the Christmas party. Annoyed with her reaction to the car, he wondered if she had turned down any of these men's gifts. Not that it was the same situation, of course. Aaron, Oleg and the others who had given her pretty things to make her smile all offered her something he never could. They were openly attempting to court Vivian while he was...

Well. What was he doing exactly? One moment, he wanted to drag her close and forever bind her to his side. The next, he pushed her away to keep her safe lest any of his enemies realize how desperately he loved her. He could only imagine how confused she was by the way he ran hot and cold with her. Hell, he was fucking confused himself!

Inside the apartment she shared with Lena, he noticed the stack of flattened moving boxes in one corner of the living room. He placed her pile of gifts on the couch and motioned toward the boxes. "So she's decided to move in with Yuri?"

"I don't think there was ever much of a decision there." Vivian peeled out of her coat, tucked the gloves into the pockets and hung it on the coat tree near the door. "You know how Yuri is when he decides he wants something. He's utterly possessive of her and hopelessly in love with her. She's head over heels for him too. I'm sure it didn't take much to convince her to move into his mansion."

"I've never seen him happier. He'll be good to her and treat her right. She will never want for anything."

"It's not the money that she wants. It's Yuri. She loves him. Like—*for real*," Vivian said definitively. "If they aren't married by next Christmas, I'll be shocked."

"Erin and Ivan too," he said, thinking of the way Ivan had confessed his plans to propose.

"Oh, yeah, definitely," Vivian agreed. "Erin thinks Ivan hung the freaking moon, and Ivan worships her. I'll call it right now. They'll be hitched by summer."

"If Ivan has his way, he'll rush her down to the courthouse or elope to Vegas to make her his wife as quickly as possible."

"I'm sure Ivan would prefer that route," she said with

a laugh. "But I know Erin. Once she starts talking wedding dresses and receptions, Ivan will just melt and give her whatever she wants. He'll make sure she has the fairytale wedding of her dreams."

He almost asked her what her dream wedding was like but caught himself. *What the hell are you thinking? Get your gift and go.*

Vivian crouched down to grab a box wrapped in shiny gold paper from under the short Christmas tree in the other corner of the living room. Holding it tight to her chest, she said, "This isn't a luxury sports car, but it's something I hope you'll love."

"Should I open it now?" He accepted the box from her and was surprised by the weight. Whatever was inside was heavy and wide.

She fluffed the bow decorating the box and shrugged. "If you want."

"I do." He tugged on the ribbon to release the knot, set aside the lid of the box and pushed apart the white tissue paper to reveal an exquisitely handcrafted scrapbook. "Did you make this?"

Unable to hide her hopeful smile, she nodded. "I took a class last fall about making books, the covers and spines and all that. I thought I would make one for us—for Samovar, I mean." She quickly corrected herself lest he get the idea that she meant for the two of them.

Putting the bottom half of the box on the couch behind him, he held the substantial scrapbook in his hands and slowly turned the pages. She had used her incredible talent to draw and paint backgrounds and captions. Divided into twelve sections, the book took him through a year's worth of celebrations.

"I left some blank pages at the back for tonight's Christmas party photos and the usual New Year's Eve celebration pics."

"This is amazing, Vee."

"It's easy to forget how many people come through the front doors at Samovar and how many of them come there to celebrate such wonderful occasions. Birthdays, engagements, weddings, baby showers, first dates—that building means a lot to so many people." She tapped a picture of a newly married couple sharing their first dance. "I want you to remember how much happiness you bring people."

The startling realization that he was the source of something so wonderful struck him hard. Every morning, he woke up feeling the weight of his responsibility to the shady underworld of Houston, and every night he went to sleep feeling as if he had done only terrible things. Now, staring him in the face, was the evidence that he wasn't as horrible as he often thought. Maybe, just maybe, there was something good within him still.

"Thank you, Vee." Voice husky with emotion, he fought the urge to lower his mouth and claim her lips in a sweet kiss. Finally tasting her would the perfect end to this tender moment. "I don't even know what to say."

"Thank you is enough."

It wasn't. It wasn't nearly enough. "You truly are the most wonderful person I have ever known."

Her lips quirked with disbelief. "When you met me, I was bleeding out in your neighbor's front yard because I had been shot and fell out of the window of a house I was trying to rob with my ex-con dad. That's hardly wonderful, Kolya."

His gut clenched so painfully at the memory of that night when little eleven-year-old Vee had crashed into his life. It was a night filled with secrets that threatened everything they now shared. It was a night that would haunt him forever.

"You know what I am, Vee. Compared to me, the few mistakes you've made are absolutely nothing." He broke his rule about touching her intimately and caressed her cheek with his knuckles. Her face registered the shock of being touched in that way, but she didn't pull away from him. In fact, she moved fractionally closer and breathed in an excited breath.

For the briefest of seconds, he seriously considered saying fuck it to the rules he had put in place to protect them both. In his mind's eye, he could see himself capturing that sweet mouth of hers and darting his tongue between her lips. Vee would grip his shirt and hold on for dear life as he kissed her with all the pent-up passion and need that had been shoved down deep and locked away within him. His love for her would ignite something primal and real between them…

And then what?

He cast aside the foolish fantasy that tempted him so cruelly. There was no way to have her and keep her safe. He refused to drag her any deeper into the terrible world she had escaped when she had survived being shot as a juvenile delinquent. Everything that was wild and innocent within her deserved a chance to blossom. The darkness that haunted him would snuff all that out like a bloom caught in an early frost.

Dragging away his hand, he stepped back and cleared his throat. "I should go. I'm sure Kostya has plans."

She smiled at him and handed him the two halves of the gift box before moving to her coat and taking out the keys to her new car. "Take these with you."

"Vee," he said warningly.

"Nikolai," she returned just as haughtily. With a daring look, she slipped the keys into the front pocket on his wool coat. It was all he could do to stifle the groan that threatened to erupt from his throat as her small hand brushed against his body. A little more to the left and she might have gotten quite an education.

He frowned down at her. "I'm not taking the car back. It's yours. It's staying out there until you come to your senses."

"Be reasonable."

"You be reasonable. You need a vehicle. I gave you a vehicle. It's that simple."

"It's anything but simple. The cost—"

"It's my money to spend however I choose, Vee. It pleases me to give you nice things."

"Why?"

Boxed into a corner, he chose his words carefully. "Because you are the most important person in the world to me."

"Me?"

"You."

She narrowed her eyes. "Not Ivan or Yuri or Dimitri or Kostya?"

"They're grown men. They're quite capable of caring for themselves."

"I'm a grown woman. I'm quite capable of taking care of myself."

"Yes, you are," he agreed. "You've accomplished so much despite everything that the world has thrown at you. This is my way of rewarding you for working so hard and achieving so much."

She opened her mouth to argue with him, but he shook his head and wagged his finger. "No more arguing tonight. We'll table this discussion for a few days. After the New Year, we'll talk."

"You mean you'll talk *at* me," she groused knowingly.

His lips slanted with amusement. "Oh, something tells me that you'll have plenty to say back to me."

Not even his closest friends dared to tell him off as often as she did. Of course, she did it with a smile and always with gentle words so it was hard to get upset with her. He had a sneaking suspicion that Vee cursing him out would probably only arouse him. That fiery side of her that he sometimes glimpsed always made him hot. He liked that she wasn't afraid of telling him what he *needed* to hear instead of what he *wanted* to hear as most people did.

She walked him to the door but stopped him before he could leave. Grasping his hand, she gave it a squeeze. "The car is beautiful, and I'm touched by the thought you put into it."

"I want you to have the very best, Vee."

"I know you do." Her gaze flicked toward the ceiling, and he spotted the sprig of mistletoe tacked above them. His breath caught in his throat as she rose on tiptoes. Certain they were playing with fire, he started to turn away from her, but every fiber of his being screamed for him to hold still and to let her have this moment.

Her soft lips brushed his cheek. It was the simplest, most innocent of kisses but it branded his skin like a searing hot iron. His eyelids briefly touched as the sweetness of her gesture raced through him, setting his body alight with need and love.

Holding himself in check, Nikolai returned the favor with a peck to the crown of her head. "*Sladkih snov.*"

She smiled up at him upon hearing the tender wish for sweet dreams. "Good night, Kolya."

Out in the cold night, he waited to hear her lock the deadbolt and doorknob and slide the chain into place. He let the rush of frigid air blow across him and chase away the agonizingly hot need burning through him. He wanted to knock on her door, tangle his fingers in her dark hair and kiss her until they were both breathless and panting. Allowing some of that weakness to win, he touched his forehead to the freezing cold door between him and the one thing he wanted more than anything in the world.

When the moment of weakness fled, he straightened up and strode out to the idling SUV. Kostya gave him a look as he placed the box on the dashboard but he didn't say anything. His confidante and right-hand man had long ago learned to read him. Kostya didn't offer unwanted opinions. It was one of the reasons Nikolai liked him so much.

They were barreling down the interstate when Kostya finally spoke. "Besian has a nice game starting in half an hour. You want to come?"

The thought of whipping the Albanian's ass in a game of cards was tempting. "Where?"

"The back room at Wet."

Nikolai lips settled into a grim line. "You know my policy on strip clubs."

"I do, but technically Wet is a gentlemen's club."

"If you say so," he grumbled, thinking of the very ungentlemanly clientele. "I've made my feelings perfectly clear on that sideline, Kostya. We don't deal in the skin trade in this family. I let you make your money with Besian in those places because you're the most loyal man I've ever had in my crew, and I've asked you to do some terrible things. I'll turn a blind eye to your involvement and thank you not to ask me to accompany you to one of those places again."

Kostya was quiet for a few seconds. "*Da*. Okay."

Stretching out his legs, Nikolai sighed. "Good."

They were pulling into the driveway of the historical

mansion Nikolai had painstakingly renovated when Kostya piped up again. "She'll come around, boss."

He glanced at his friend. "To?"

"The car," Kostya clarified. "She's in a strange position. You're her boss. People already talk."

He went rigid. "What people? What are they saying?"

Kostya shrugged. "Some of the other girls at the restaurant. Some of the old-timers who hang around at lunch. Some of the men in the crews. They see what you've done for her. They...speculate."

"Speculate? About what?"

"You know."

"I don't."

Kostya seemed reluctant to say the words. "They talk about Vivian being your mistress."

Nikolai had no doubt that Kostya used a nicer word than others were throwing about. "The next time someone says something like about Vivian, you send them to me and I'll straighten them out. She isn't that sort of woman. She's *good*."

Kostya held up both hands. "I'm just trying to help you understand why Vivian is so leery about accepting the car. It's not easy for her."

"I never meant—I've only ever wanted to make life better for her, to give her things that she deserves."

"At some point, you have to choose. You can't be her protector forever. If she falls in love with another man, it won't work. So you had better decide what you want with her and make your move. Otherwise..."

He understood what Kostya was saying. "It's not that simple. You know it's not that easy. My position here is dangerous. The people close to me are the most vulnerable."

"She's already vulnerable. Her father is Romero

Valero. It doesn't get much more dangerous than that, boss."

He conceded that Kostya had a point. "It's not the right time."

"Is it ever?" His friend held his gaze. "You've seen what Vanya, Dima and Yuri have now. You could have that with Vivian."

"I've also seen how close my friends came to losing their women." The vision of a bound Lena and stabbed Yuri flashed before him. He glanced at his clean hands but could see the phantom stain of so much blood on them. "I can't risk her. She's everything to me."

"And what about what she wants?"

Nikolai's gaze snapped to Kostya's face. "What do you mean?"

"I mean that you haven't factored what Vivian wants into your decision. She's part of the equation. Her opinion matters."

"She's too young to know what she wants."

Kostya snorted. "God, I want to be there when you tell her that. It will be epic."

He frowned at the cleaner. "Don't you have a poker game to attend?"

"I do once you get the hell out of my SUV."

Chuckling roughly at Kostya's rude retort, Nikolai gathered his things and opened the door. "I think I like you better when you're silent and brooding. This other you? The driver's seat psychologist? He's fucking annoying."

Kostya laughed hard. "Get out. Go inside. Feel sorry yourself."

"I hope you lose everything at the table tonight."

Kostya shot him the finger, and Nikolai slammed the door shut. Grinning at their uncouth behavior, he entered his house, grabbed a beer from the refrigerator and moved to his library. He kicked off his shoes, peeled out of his tie and rolled up his sleeves. Comfortable in one of the reading chairs, he adjusted the light behind him and opened the scrapbook.

Sipping his beer, he thought of how much work Vivian had put into the gift. He let his finger drift along the design she had drawn on a baby shower page. Her smiling face had been caught in the snapshot as she brought out a silly diaper-shaped cake for the mother-to-be. Even with her hair in a ponytail and wearing the rather plain-looking waitress uniform, Vivian took his breath away. His finger circled her face.

Closing his eyes, he remembered the heat of her lips against his skin. Was Kostya right? Was it time to ask Vivian what she wanted? Was he brave enough to bear the possible rejection? If she wanted him—unlikely as that was—would she have the courage to stand at his side, or would she flee at the first sign of danger?

Danger…

A sixth sense told him trouble was coming. Houston had been quiet for far too long. He had no doubt that some new and violent outburst would rock the underworld. A whisper soft threat told him he would get his answer about Vivian's courage soon enough.

As to the rest? He trusted that Vivian had been thrown into his life that muggy April night for a reason. Whatever it was, the answer would come in time. Until then? Well. He was a patient man—and she was worth the wait.

You can read Nikolai and Vivian's story in NIKOLAI (Her Russian Protector #4) available now in ebook and print and coming soon in audiobook! Nikolai and Vivian will also be featured in a novel-length sequel to be released in Spring 2014.

NINE LADIES DANCING
KOSTYA

Taking the front entrance of the strip club where he was co-owner, Kostya Antonovich nodded at the two bouncers manning the door. Once inside the newly remodeled space, he let his eyes adjust to the dimmer lighting. The renovation project had cost them an outrageous amount of money but already they were seeing an uptick in business. The world-class décor and first-rate entertainment allowed them to charge higher prices too.

With the recent loosening of restrictions and a hefty annual fee, the entertainers were allowed to dance topless again within the city limits. That meant no pasties and no latex—and the men couldn't get enough. An advertising campaign with some cheeky slogans and plenty of drink and dance specials were pushing men through the doors and keeping the girls busy. Bachelor party bookings were up, and online inquiries about private parties for upcoming business conventions were through the roof.

No doubt about it, the next year was going to be very, very good for business.

"Mr. Antonovich!" Cherish, one of the hostesses, grinned warmly and ran her hand up his arm. "I wondered if we would see you tonight. Would you like me to send the usual to the back room?"

"Please," he said, and deftly slipped her a tip. Glancing around the establishment, he noticed a handful of the girls giggling together at the bar and ignoring the customers. Though he didn't relish being a mean bastard, this was a business and it existed for one reason—to make money. "Get those girls to work—or send them home."

"Yes, sir."

Crossing the floor, he eyed the nine dancers entertaining the heavy crowd. It had been Besian's idea to do a play on the Christmas carol as part of their advertising. It looked to be working, especially with girls all decked out in red and green tinsel and Santa hats.

His gaze settled on the main stage where Sapphire, one of the club's most popular dancers, whipped her blonde hair and gyrated wildly against the pole. Her dark skin had been dusted with enough glitter to highlight her voluptuous curves. He wasn't at all surprised to see the money piling up on the stage. Thighs wide open, she crouched down to let the men get an extremely up close view of all her womanly secrets.

There were nights when Kostya felt sorry for himself, when he acknowledged that his cold and empty existence was one that most people would find unbearable, but then he would spend an evening at one of his strip clubs and realize that his life wasn't nearly so bad. Here it was, Christmas Eve, and these pathetic losers were bellied up to a mirrored stage staring at a woman who wouldn't give them the time of day if not for the cash gripped in their hands. They ought to be home with their families or friends but no. They were here in this soulless place.

As much as he liked to taunt Nikolai, he envied the man for his stance on these types of establishments and on the skin trade. Unlike a lot of the men who ran in their circles, Nikolai had principles. There were lines the boss didn't cross, especially when it came to exploiting women or children, so strip clubs were never a part of the family's earning portfolio.

That wasn't to say they didn't deal in some shady fucking shit. Guns, narcotics, black market pharmaceuticals—they dabbled in plenty of illicit earning waters but never, *ever* prostitution. It was a strange line to draw considering the underbelly they inhabited but it wasn't up for discussion. Nikolai laid down the law, and everyone else toed the line—or Kostya and Sergei visited them.

These days, the boss seemed intent on forcing them into cleaner, less risky income streams. He sensed Nikolai had a plan brewing, but the boss would keep those cards very close to the chest until it was time to make a move. Kostya didn't mind the secrecy because he trusted he would be the first to find out when Nikolai was ready. Until then, Kostya was happy not to have another secret burdening him. God knew he had enough to keep track of these days.

"Kostya!" Besian bellowed a greeting from his spot at the card table. Judging by the half-empty bottle of *raki* sitting in front of the Albanian mob captain and the pile of chips, the man was having a hell of a good night.

"I see you started without me." He tried to get a peek at the other players' cards as he moved to the open seat but only caught a glimpse of Sergei's. Seeing the enforcer's hand, he was glad to have missed this round. It looked like Nikolai's bare-knuckle champion was about to clean out the Albanian captain.

"Drink?" Besian wiggled the bottle of plum-flavored liquor before splashing some into his own glass.

Kostya held out his hand and shook his head. "They're bringing me a beer."

As if on cue, a scantily clad waitress arrived with a tray of drinks. Water for Sergei, vodka and whisky for the men from Besian's camp and an ice cold Shiner 97 for him. He made sure to tip the girl who brought in their drinks before taking a sip. Glancing around the room, he nudged Sergei. "Where's Danny?"

Sergei shrugged, his gaze never leaving his cards. "Playing Santa Claus, I suspect."

"Huh?" Kostya sat back, lit up a cigarette and watched the game play out in front of him. The rest of the table folded as Sergei raised the stakes and Besian stupidly blundered right into the trap.

"Those kids next door," the behemoth explained. "I think he has a crush on the big sister. He swears up and down there's nothing to it but..."

He thought about the townhouse where Danny lived. He'd been there once or twice and vaguely remembered the family that lived there. "That's the dad with the drinking problem, yeah?"

"Yeah." Sergei glanced at Besian. "He's on the books at the Black Eagle."

"What's his name?" Besian asked upon hearing the name of the social club where the Albanian loan shark Afrim Barisha took bets.

"Bill? Bob? No." Sergei seemed to be thinking. "Burt?"

"Yeah. Yeah. I know this one. He's fat? Bald? He's a good customer. He usually pays on time and keeps coming back."

Kostya made a mental note to keep an eye on that situation. Danila was only twenty-three or twenty-four. He was still young enough to think he could save the whole fucking world. The last thing the kid needed was to get caught up in a mess while playing the hero for some pretty young girl.

Somehow Danny had managed to remain untouched by the darkness of their world. He hadn't yet been asked to do something truly violent for the family—but his time was coming. Sooner or later, they all spilled blood.

Kostya grinned when Sergei dropped his cards and Besian let loose a string of Albanian curse words. Sweeping his winnings toward him, the fighter neatly stacked his chips. Kostya bought his way into the game and sized up his opponents. He was good, but Besian and Sergei were better. Setting a mental limit, Kostya made up his mind to get out of the game when he hit that number.

For next two hours, he bullshitted and played cards. He enjoyed watching Sergei win round after round, especially since he knew how much the other man needed that money to get his brother and mother over here from Russia. When he was in the hole a month's salary, Kostya bowed out of the game.

"Deal me out this round," Besian instructed before rising from his seat. "Let me walk you out, Kostya."

He knew that tone. Besian had a piece of information he wanted to share discreetly. "Sure."

Shoulder to shoulder, they left the back room and ended up in the hallway there. Besian looked up and down the hall before lowering his voice. "One of my guys locked up in Beaumont got me a message about a certain machete-wielding psycho."

Machete-wielding psycho? There was only one man

who fit that bill—and he was Vivian Valero's father. "Romero?"

"The one and only," Besian confirmed.

"What's he up to?"

"He's talking to the Feds."

"Which ones?"

"The Marshals."

Kostya didn't like the sound of that. There was only one reason a man like Romero would talk to that group, and it was an incredibly dangerous one.

"I know that Nikolai has…," the Albanian seemed to be choosing his words carefully, "…a soft spot for the daughter. If her old man is thinking about turning against his cartel or his outlaw crew? It won't be good for her."

That was putting it mildly. "I'll let the boss know. He'll appreciate the heads-up."

"I'm counting on it." Besian smiled slyly. "One good turn…"

He chuckled softly. "Yes. I'm sure he'll be happy to repay the favor someday."

Leaving Besian, he headed out of the strip club, stopping only long enough to drop tips on the satellite stages for the dancers who weren't getting much attention. The crowd was thinning, and the girls who weren't as popular were going to have a hard time making much money tonight.

"You leaving already, baby?" Sapphire sidled up close to him. Like most of the entertainers, she wore too much perfume and too much makeup. She was a beautiful woman beneath all that, but the men who frequented the establishment expected a certain look. It was all about providing a fantasy, and Sapphire understood the theater element better than most.

"It's late."

"Not that late, honey." Her hand glided down his chest and along the flat plank of his stomach to cup his cock. Though he wasn't interested in her like that, his body nonetheless reacted to her skilled touch. "I can think of a reason to stay out tonight."

"I have somewhere else to be." He carefully removed her groping hand from his body. "You know my rules. I don't date the employees."

"That's a shame, sugar." She patted his chest. "You're a curiosity I would love to satisfy."

"I'm flattered, but I'm not your man, sweetheart."

He disentangled himself from the gorgeous dancer and left the club. His body's reaction to her touch annoyed him. Not because he had gotten hard but because of the smiling face of a different woman that had flashed before him. *Her.* God, of all the fucking women in the world, why did it have to be *her* that made his chest tighten and his cock stand at attention?

Refusing to think about Holly Phillips, he started his SUV. Driving home, he couldn't help but think of all the free pussy he declined night after night. Between the four clubs he owned with Besian in the greater Houston area, there was always some dancer trying to seduce him. While his partner often sampled the endless buffet of women, Kostya preferred to find his dates elsewhere.

His position as Nikolai's right hand man seemed to draw women to him but for all the wrong reasons. The tattoos always brought out the questions. What was he supposed to say?

Oh, I got this one after I committed my first robbery. Yeah, this dagger was my first hit—but not with the mob. This one I gave myself to commemorate the end of my government contract. This one marks me as Nikolai's man. That one marks me as a cleaner.

There would be two reactions to that sort of honesty.

The smart women would scream and run away from him, and the crazy ones who were aroused by danger and violence would attach themselves to him like a parasite, always wanting more gruesome details.

No, it was much simpler to just keep to himself. Now that he was staring forty in the face, Kostya had begun to accept his fate. He had made choices in his life, some out of necessity and others more calculated, that had forever closed certain doors to him. He was too dark inside, too stained with sin, to ever be loved by a good woman.

And, anyway, if he didn't catch a bullet by fifty, he would be shocked. There was no use in dreaming of things he simply couldn't have. He wasn't Ivan. He wasn't getting out of Nikolai's family. There would be no sweet, gentle woman like Erin to save him.

His thoughts turned to Vivian and this shit brewing with her father. The situation had trouble written all over it. As he pulled into his driveway and waited for his garage door to rise, he flashed back to the night Vivian had nearly died in Nikolai's arms. She had been the scrawniest little thing back then. No one looking at her as a child could ever have imagined how she would blossom into such a hauntingly beautiful young woman. It was no surprise that she had bewitched Nikolai with those sky blue eyes of hers.

Getting out of his vehicle, he decided he would have one last smoke before heading inside. He had been trying to cut back and was doing quite well, but the poker game had whet his appetite for the jolt of nicotine. Letting the garage door close behind him, Kostya leaned against the side of his house and simply stared out across his quiet, still neighborhood.

It amazed him that he was able to blend in so easily with the rest of his middle class neighbors. He had chosen the modest ranch-style home for that very reason. He wanted to live invisibly, to be the man everyone waved at when he retrieved his mail or the morning paper but also the man no one knew. The few neighbors who asked got the same answer. *I'm a security consultant.*

Only Holly had ever dared to ask more questions. Only she had tempted him to break his number one rule. *Don't get involved.* He repeated it to himself again and again.

Unsettled by the way she affected him, Kostya tried to figure out what it was about his petite blonde-haired neighbor that caused his stomach to leap and his chest to buzz whenever she was near. Oh, Holly was pretty, but he saw beautiful women every day and none of them made him feel like that. She had a nice laugh but so did plenty of other women. Her figure was a bit slim for his usual tastes. He had always preferred big, lush breasts and a nice, heavy ass not that pixie-like build she sported.

Fishing his lighter and cigarettes from his pocket, he started to light up but held off when he spotted the two headlights illuminating the street. Nosiness went naturally with his occupation. Safe in the shadows and well hidden, he watched the pricey sedan roll down the cul-de-sac lane. He didn't recognize the vehicle as one that belonged to any of his neighbors. On alert, he shifted his hand back to his holstered weapon. It wouldn't be the first time someone had ordered a hit on a rival outfit during the holidays.

When the car swung around and slid up against the sidewalk lining Holly's house, his body went stiff. A surge of something that felt suspiciously like jealousy tore through him. *Settle the fuck down*, he silently ordered himself. *She's not yours. She can never be yours.*

Wanting to make sure she got inside all right—and wanting to get a good look at the man who had brought her home—Kostya jammed his cigarettes and lighter back into his pocket and crept around the edge of his garage. He made sure to stay cloaked by the darkness.

When the passenger side door opened, Holly's angry, upset voice filtered into the night. Instantly, his jaw tightened. Before he could stop himself, he was cutting across his yard to rescue her. From what, he didn't know yet, but the sound of a man shouting at her enraged him.

"You're a pig!" Sobbing loudly, Holly clambered out of the sedan and dragged her coat along the wet sidewalk. The sleeve of her pretty gold dress was torn, revealing the strap of her red bra. Any other time that tempting view of her silky flesh might have tripped him up but right now it infuriated him.

"Yeah? Well you're a frigid fucking bitch!" A second later, her shiny metallic clutch was launched out of the vehicle and whacked her right in the face. "Whore!"

Holly cried out in pain and fell to her knees on the brittle, cold grass.

Seeing red, Kostya stormed to the driver's side door and jerked it open. The driver, a blond in his early thirties gaped up at him in shock. Kostya reached down, unlatched the asshole's seatbelt and hauled him right out of the driver's seat. Slamming her date against the car, he used his larger body to trap the man in place.

Don't kill him. Not in front of Holly. Don't let her see the monster inside you.

Maintaining the thinnest hold on the vicious beast within him, Kostya decided not to use the knife sheathed against his boot or the pistol holstered under his jacket. There were other ways of hurting a man. Much, much more painful ways…

He gripped the dirty bastard's balls in a tight clench. The man let loose a pitiful whine. "Did you just call my friend a whore?" The man whimpered as Kostya squeezed harder. "Huh?"

"I-I-I," the man stammered unintelligibly.

He knocked into the asshole with his shoulder. "Man the fuck up and answer me!"

"I didn't mean it." The bastard actually looked like he was about to start crying. Revulsion raced through Kostya. Weak. Pathetic. Loser.

Movement near the hood of the car filtered through his hazy red vision. Holding her clutch in both hands, Holly stared on with wide eyes. Streaks of mascara ran down her face. The sight of her ripped dress made him want to crush this bastard's balls. "Kostya?"

Pushing his forearm against the man's throat, Kostya sucked in a steadying breath. He held Holly's terrified gaze. "Did he hit you?"

She quickly shook her head, those long blonde tresses swishing around her shoulders. "No. I mean—not until he threw this at me." She gingerly rubbed her reddened nose and scratched cheek.

The urge to beat the man bloody was strong. Not wanting to make such a big mess in her front yard, he decided to give the fucker a taste of his own medicine. Eyeing her clutch, he ordered. "Bring it to me, Holly."

She swallowed nervously before walking toward him. He snatched the clutch from her hand, took a quick step back and smacked the bastard right across the face with it. With a backhand movement, he slapped the man again, making sure to catch the metal closure against her date's skin. If Holly was going to bleed, so was this loser.

"Oh my god!" Holly gasped with shock, and the sniveling little shit in front of him started to sob hysterically.

"Did you like that?"

"N-n-no!" The guy cringed and lifted his shoulders in a bracing move, as if he expected to be hit again.

Kostya considered it but didn't think he could keep his bloodthirsty instincts in check much longer. "Do you think she enjoyed being hit with it?"

"No."

"Maybe I should follow you home, tear your clothes and call you names in your front yard. Would you like that?"

"No. Please!"

Disgusted by the pathetic excuse for a man in front of him, he released his hold and shoved the man against his vehicle. "Get the fuck out of here. *Now.*" Stepping close, he hissed, "If I ever find out that you so much as look at Holly again, I'll fucking come for you."

The guy's panicked gaze flitted along the tattoos exposed on Kostya's neck. He was stupid, but he wasn't *that* stupid. "I won't. She'll never see me again."

"I'm holding you to that." He pushed the man into the front seat. "Go."

Shaking and crying, the asshole shut his door. Kostya grabbed Holly's hand and dragged her safely behind him as her date from hell punched the gas and spun his tires. He tore down their street and disappeared.

Concerned for her, Kostya pivoted quickly, cupped her face and tilted back her head. He gazed at the injury. "We have to put ice on that."

Dazed, she clutched his wrist, her soft fingers curling along his skin and setting his body alight with need. "Thank you."

Teased by the scent of her perfume, Kostya dropped his gaze to her pink lips. Perhaps he could have just one kiss…?

No. Don't be stupid. Get her inside. Go home.

Clearing his throat, he took his hand away from her face. "You don't have to thank me for helping you." He spotted the goose bumps rising along her exposed skin. A cold wind blew across them. He picked up her jacket and draped it around her shoulders. "Let's get you inside before you freeze to death."

Not arguing with him, Holly led him up her sidewalk and into her home. Their floor plans were similar with his house only slightly larger. Where he had chosen a dark hickory for his floors, she had picked out a pale, gleaming oak. Her walls were a breezy shade of blue and bedecked with photos and witty word art pieces.

The differences in their lives had never been more perfectly presented to him. She was sweet, fun and lived a full, happy life. He was dark, somber and lived a life filled with terrible secrets and even worse deeds.

Shaking off that depressing thought, he said, "Go change. I'll make an ice pack for your face."

"Oh, Kostya, you don't have to do that." Embarrassment caused her ears to flush. "You did enough coming to my rescue out there with Cody."

He committed the other man's name to memory along with the license plate on the car. He fully intended to pay Cody a visit in a few days just to rattle that bastard's cage. "Where the hell did you meet someone like that?"

"His mom comes to the salon. She's friends with my mother. I guess they thought it would be a good idea to set us up. You know, the flighty cosmetologist with the successful divorce lawyer. He had tickets for the Weston Christmas Gala so I accepted the date thinking he might have some potential."

What about me? Does she think I have potential? No, he silently acknowledged. He had been friend-zoned from their very first meeting nearly a year earlier. For her safety, it was best.

"He's scum, Holly."

"He was just a little drunk and really stupid."

"I've been very drunk and extremely stupid, but I've never put my hands on a woman." He flexed his fingers at his sides rather than indulge the clawing need within him to caress her bare skin. "Men like that are dangerous. You will never go out with that man again. Do you understand?"

"Excuse me?" Her green eyes went wide with surprise at his harsh tone. "You're my friend, but you don't get to tell me how to live my life."

"Because I am your friend, I get to tell you all sorts of things that you don't want to hear, Holly. That man is off-limits. He'll hurt you—and then I'll have to hurt him."

Her expression relaxed some. "I appreciate you looking out for me, but you don't have to go all crazy alpha male on me. You know? You could just say, 'Hey, Holly, you can do better.' You don't have to throw down ultimatums."

Duly chastised, he nodded. "You can do better, Holly. Much, much better," he murmured. "You deserve the very best in a man. Not some fucking prick like that."

"Well, when you find that man, send him my way." With a soft touch to his chest, she said, "There's beer in my fridge. Make yourself comfortable. I'll be back in a few minutes."

Unable to help himself, he tilted his head and watched the sultry swing of her trim hips as she walked down the hall to the master suite. For a moment, he let himself imagine what it would be like to be a true knight in shining armor riding to the rescue of his woman. A real hero wouldn't be standing here in her living room, tiny purse in hand, while the damsel in distress disappeared into a bedroom.

The sexiest images taunted him. If he was a good man, a man who could offer Holly a future, he would follow her down that hall, gather her tightly in his arms and finally get that kiss he had wanted since meeting her on that rainy March morning. Maybe it would go somewhere. Maybe it wouldn't. Either way, he would finally quench the undeniable thirst for that sweet, pouty mouth of hers.

Rolling his neck, Kostya cursed himself for even dreaming of something so wildly impossible. She inhabited a world so far removed from his it was as if they lived on opposite ends of the known universe.

Turning toward her kitchen, he came face to face with dozens of framed photographs arranged gallery style on her walls. As if to prove a point, the wall mocked him. She had family and friends who loved her. What did he have? He had Nikolai's family, all of them bonded by a different sort of blood.

Stepping closer to inspect the photos, he placed her clutch on the entryway table and scanned the ones he had already seen the half a dozen or so times he had been inside her home. They provided a snapshot of her life in Houston. Holly as a cheerleader at a high school football game. Holly as the Prom Queen. Holly at sorority parties. Holly graduating from Rice. Holly opening the salon with her two best friends.

He enjoyed the photos of Holly and her mother the most. He hadn't met Annette Martin yet, but she looked like a very nice woman. Judging by her age in the newest photos, she had been an older mother, probably in her early forties when Holly was born. He wondered if that was why she had chosen to raise Holly alone and without the help of a husband or partner. By all accounts, Annette was quite successful in her career with one of Houston's mega energy firms. She was now a CFO and incredibly well-respected.

"Are you ogling me in my cheerleader uniform again?"

Kostya laughed and made the mistake of glancing at her. Though he had just come from a strip club where the women were walking around bare ass naked, it was the sight of Holly in slim-fitting yoga pants and a plain pink T-shirt that made his cock stir to life. Fresh faced, she had wiped away all the traces of her makeup and pulled her blonde hair into a ponytail.

Ignoring that pulsing ache deep in his belly, Kostya shook his head. "No, I wasn't ogling you."

"Sure you weren't, you perv," she teased and bumped him with her hip.

He didn't even try to stop the smile that curved his typically grim-set mouth. Sliding his gaze along the wall, he spotted a set of photos he had never seen. He was a bit taken aback by the Russian landmarks he knew only too well. "Those are new."

"Yes." She reached out to trace the frames. "Mom is going to downsize in the spring from that monstrosity of a mansion up in The Woodlands so we've been going through the rooms at the house to see what she'll keep, sell or donate. I found a box of photographs from her year in Russia."

"What was she doing there?" He glanced at the pictures of Annette around various tourist hotspots like the Hermitage Museum and Saint Basil's Cathedral.

"The company she works for wanted to get in on the ground level of the oil and gas exploration over there. She hopped around the country and spent most of her time in Kazakhstan, I guess. It was only the last three months or so that she was in Moscow and St. Petersburg."

As he studied the photos, a conclusion began to form. He noted the fashions her mother wore, the vehicles and even the few visible advertisements. It wasn't difficult to do the math. "Your father...?"

"Yes," Holly said quietly. "Before you ask, no, I don't know his name. Mom said it's not important, and frankly, I decided that I didn't want to know the name of the man who wanted nothing to do with me or my mother."

Kostya wondered if it was that simple. Not wanting to upset her, he let the issue drop. He had his own ways of finding out information like that.

"Come on. Let's have that beer." She gave the sleeve of his jacket a tug. "Take this off. You're going to burn up in here under all that leather."

"I'm fine." He didn't want to be forced to reveal the gun hidden under his jacket. When they reached the kitchen, he stopped her before she got to the refrigerator. "I'll get that. You get up here." He patted the granite counter. "Let me get a look at that scrape on your cheek."

"I've already put some antibiotic ointment on it."

"I still want to look at it. You might need to be seen by a doctor."

She rolled her eyes at him. "You are way too overprotective."

He bit back a reply and grabbed two beers from the fridge. She hopped up onto the small island and impatiently swung her legs while he filled a small plastic bag with ice and wrapped it with a dishtowel.

Standing in front of her, he set aside the ice pack and gingerly clasped her face between his hands. Their gazes clashed as he tilted her head back and examined the grazed skin across the tip of her nose and the apple of her cheek. It took all the self-control he could muster not to gently caress her beautiful face and run his thumb along that bee-stung lower lip.

"You'll have a bruise." Fingertips electrified by the contact with her supple skin, he reached for the ice pack. "It won't be too bad."

"Thankfully, I'm an ace at makeup application." She took the pack from him and placed it against her puffy cheek. She turned a critical eye to the front of his shirt. "Although, maybe I should come to you for tips if I ever have a hankering to toss on some stripper dust."

He glanced down and saw the glittery specks on the front of his shirt. "Shit."

She laughed and gestured toward the beers. "Grab the church key from the fridge and pop that top for me. I'll definitely need a drink for this story."

"There's no story." He swiped the magnet-backed bottle opener from the stainless steel door.

"Really? Because I'm thinking that a handsome guy like you hanging out in some dirty freaking strip club on Christmas Eve has got to have a story behind it."

Hearing her call him handsome made his heartbeat speed up. Popping the caps off the beers, he handed one to her. "First, Wet isn't a dirty freaking strip club." He repeated her exact phrase. "It's a first-rate gentlemen's club."

"If you say so…" She sipped her beer.

"I do."

"But why?"

"Why what?"

"Why were you there? Surely, you have no problem finding a hot woman willing to dance naked in your own bedroom."

He nearly choked on his mouthful of beer. Gulping it down, he glanced at her to see if she was teasing him. She looked dead serious. Clearing his throat, he stated, "I don't bring women to my house."

"I noticed that."

"Did you?" He wasn't sure he liked being watched that closely. "Well, I've noticed you don't have overnight guests either."

"By the time we shut the salon down, it's almost nine. Then I've got to drive across town, make dinner, do laundry, blah, blah, blah." She waved her hand. "Trying to get a small business through the first five years is tough. And, obviously, after tonight's front yard spectacle, I've got no business inviting men home with me."

He wasn't sure if she expected him to encourage her to try again. If she did, she was shit out of luck because he wasn't about to suggest anything of the sort. Selfish as it was, he didn't want any man heating up her sheets.

Unless it's me.

Pushing aside that tempting thought, he asked, "How is business?"

She smiled knowingly before taking another drink. Mercifully, she let the topic of strip clubs go and didn't force him to admit that he owned them. They finished their beers while chatting about the salon she loved so much. With her mother's deep pockets funding the enterprise, they were very nearly in the black. Considering the unbelievable amount of hours Holly had put into her salon, he was thrilled for her. She deserved so much success.

"I should go." He said after draining the last of his drink. "It's late. You need to rest."

"I need a lot of things," she murmured, "but I'm not sure rest is at the top of that list."

Was she coming onto him? He couldn't tell and didn't want to risk misreading her and upsetting their friendship.

"Well, I'm an old man so rest is at the top of mine."

"Oh, please." She rolled her eyes. "What are you? Thirty-four? Thirty-five?"

"Thirty-seven."

"Seriously?" She slanted her head to the side and examined him more closely. "You're going to be one of those ridiculously sexy silver foxes in another twenty years."

He chortled loudly and swiped the empty bottle from her hand. "You're drunk."

"Hardly," she said and hopped down off the island. "I've only had a glass of wine and that beer all night."

"You're a lightweight." In his line of work, accurately judging height and weight came in very handy. Holly couldn't weigh more than fifty kilograms. Maybe fifty-two, he allowed, while rinsing their empty bottles in the sink. He dropped them into the recycling bin in her laundry room and came back into the kitchen to find she had disappeared on him.

Frowning, he went in search of her. He found Holly crouched down in front of her Christmas tree. There were only a handful of presents under the tree, and she selected a gift bag with a vintage holiday print on the front. Grinning at him, she crossed the living room and presented it to him. "So, I know we agreed we were going to trade white elephant gifts this year…"

He narrowed his eyes at her. "But?"

"But I decided to get you something a little silly and something else that I think you'll actually enjoy."

He decided not to ruin her surprise because he had done the same thing for her. Instead, he exhaled dramatically. "I suppose I will let it slide this year."

She raised an eyebrow and saucily retorted, "Or I could bend over the arm of that couch and you could give my backside a swat for being such a naughty little elf."

Heat unfurled fast and hard in his core. The vision of her bare, wiggling ass enticed him. What would her bottom look like all pink and hot after a good spanking? He could almost feel her snug, wet heat wrapped around his cock while he fucked her roughly after giving her exactly what she deserved—and needed.

Taking the bag from her, he warned, "You should be careful making overtures like that, Holly. One of these days, a man might take you up on them."

She smiled at him. "Oh, I'm counting on it."

The thought of another man accepting her offer made his stomach lurch. The overpowering urge to cup that perky little ass of hers and drag her tight to his chest was almost too much to deny. Right here, right now, he could claim her as his woman. For tonight, at least, he could be an everyday sort of man making love to and enjoying the woman of his dreams.

But it wasn't that simple.

Because you aren't an everyday sort of man. You're a mob cleaner and a hit man. You're all wrong for Holly. Let her go. Let her have the chance to find the man she deserves.

Taking the gift bag from her, he stepped back before the scent and heat of her coaxed him to make a huge mistake. "Thank you, Holly."

"No, thank you, Kostya. You saved me tonight."

"If you see Cody again—"

"I'll tell you," she promised. "But I don't think either one of us will ever see him again."

For Cody's sake, Kostya hoped that was true.

Holly shadowed him to the front door. "Good night, Kostya. Merry Christmas."

"Merry Christmas, Holly." He stepped onto the welcome mat and gestured to her door. "Lock up."

"There you go again with your overprotectiveness."

"Someone has to look out for you."

"So it may as well be you?"

He nodded. "Yes."

She smiled sweetly. "I can't imagine a better protector."

Oh, if only she knew…

"Night."

"*Spokoynoy nochi.*"

Safe inside his house, Kostya carried the gift bag into his kitchen and shrugged out of his jacket. He peeled off his holster and placed his pistol on the counter next to the present. After plucking free the knife sheathed along his left leg and his backup pistol from the right, he pulled the fluffy red and green tissue paper out of the bag and withdrew his gift.

His fingers brushed something cold and hard. Ceramic? He felt another object of the same size next to it. He grabbed one and hauled it out of the bag. Staring at the bizarre and slightly creepy face looking right back at him, Kostya burst out with laughter. It was a garden gnome!

He found the female match to the pair inside the bag and placed her next to the white-bearded male gnome. The homeowner's association would hit him hard for putting them in his front yard, but Kostya didn't care. He wanted Holly to laugh every time she pulled into her driveway and spotted the weird miniatures in the flower beds in front of his house.

Remembering the real gift she had admitted to buying him, he fished around in the bag and finally withdrew a card. He opened the envelope and found a gift certificate to the very last place he had ever expected—the animal shelter. Wondering what in the world she had been thinking, he read the note scrawled inside the card.

Because I know you're going to hem-and-haw over this, it's good for a year. Oh—and I get first dibs on helping you name your new furry friend. I've already got a shortlist. What do you think about Tokarev?

He traced the loopy shapes of her handwriting. A dog? Was she insane? That was the very last thing he needed.

Except.

Well.

Maybe it would be nice to have a companion.

Maybe.

Possibly.

Even as he mentally listed all the reasons why a dog was a terrible idea, he grudgingly admitted that Tokarev would be a good name for his pet, especially considering his fondness for the surplus 7.62x25 ammunition that he occasionally got his hands on during the family's illicit arms trading.

Leaving the gift certificate on the counter, he walked over to the small dining room table where Holly's gift sat. Unlike her, he hadn't decorated for Christmas and didn't have a tree. She had been the only person he had shopped for this year.

In fact, she was the only person he had shopped for since his mother's death over ten years ago.

Though he had planned to drop off her gift in the morning, he decided that he wanted to have a little fun with her tonight. There was no chimney for him to come crashing down so her front door would have to do.

Not bothering with his jacket, he nonetheless tucked a pistol into the back of his jeans. Out in the cold, wet night, he made a stealth crossing of their property lines and walked up to her front door. He could see the faint glow of a television around the closed wooden blinds and the edges of her living room drapes. He placed his gift on the welcome mat, rang the doorbell—and ran like a kid pulling a prank.

He made it to the tree in her front yard before she opened the door. He could only just make out her silhouette in the light shining behind her. She bent down to pick up the gift and then glanced around the yard. Feeling sillier than he had in years, Kostya deepened his voice and called out, "Ho, ho, ho!"

Holly's snort of laughter echoed in the quiet night. "Aw, Santa, you shouldn't have! Bacon flavored toothpaste in a jewelry box? I'm such a lucky girl."

He chuckled but remained hidden behind the tree. "Don't throw away that jewelry box without turning it over first."

"Why? Is there—holy shit! Kostya, this is too much."

He smiled at the thought of her wearing the gold bracelet with the jade cabochon that he had carefully taped to the bottom of the box. The moment he had seen the bracelet in the jeweler's case, he had thought of her pretty green eyes. "Santa doesn't have the receipt so you'll have to keep it."

She didn't say anything for a few seconds, and he started to worry. Had he been wrong to give her jewelry? He had been sure that a bracelet was the perfect gift for her. Now he had second thoughts.

"Santa will have to let me cook him dinner to show my appreciation."

Relieved that she liked the gift, he replied, "Santa will have to check his calendar and get back to you. Now—go back inside and lock that door."

"Yeah. Okay. Bossy butt."

He laughed again and waited for the front door to close before returning to his house. Alone in his bedroom sometime later, Kostya stared at the ceiling and played his moments with Holly on an endless loop inside his head. It struck him suddenly that she had given him the greatest gift of all this Christmas.

She had given him a glimpse of what it might be like to be normal, and—God help him—he liked it. One taste of how things could be if he wasn't mired in the swamp of his mobbed-up life, and Kostya craved the possibilities.

Was this the feeling that Ivan Markovic and Alexei Sarnov had chased all those years ago when they were making their exit plans? Now, Ivan had everything he wanted—a clean life, a successful business and a gorgeous woman who loved him.

Can I have that?

He honestly didn't know. Even before getting involved with Nikolai's crew, Kostya had never dared to dream that his life might be normal. His rather unorthodox upbringing with parents who were KGB operatives had sealed that deal. When he had proven to be a genius like them, he had gone to university where he had excelled in biochemistry and then he had accepted a government contract to follow in his parents' footsteps.

Getting out from under the Kremlin's thumb had required that he make a hasty exit from his homeland, and there had been only one way to do it—Maksim Prokhorov, the mob boss of Moscow. Through the boss' vast network, Kostya had ended up here and attached to Nikolai. His friendship with Nikolai was the truest of his life, and he would give his life to defend his friend and his boss.

But what if there was something else for him?

Even if he could get out—and the odds of him surviving such a move were less than one percent—what the hell could he offer a woman like Holly?

Money wasn't an issue. He had so much of it stashed away in various banks and hidey holes around the world that he could stop working tomorrow and live the life of a very rich man until he was ninety years old. She could have anything she wanted if she belonged to him.

But what if she wanted more than he could give? If she started asking hard questions about his life and his work, could he tell her the truth? What would she say if she found out about the dark, unforgiveable things he had done in the past? His particular skillset lent itself to some truly terrible deeds.

Rolling onto his stomach, Kostya punched his pillow into submission and clamped his eyes shut. He didn't want to think of all the reasons why he couldn't have what he wanted. Tomorrow, in the cold light of day, he would accept the reality of his totally fucking shit situation. Tonight, in his dreams, he could have the woman he wanted. He could have Holly Phillips.

In a bikini, on a beach, and throwing a Frisbee with a mutt of a dog named Tokarev, he decided with a sly smile. It was Christmas after all. He might as well dream big!

You can read all about Kostya finally having a chance at his happily ever after in Spring 2014!

TOYS FOR TOTS
DANILA

As if on an army recon mission, Danila Cherevin slowly drove through the parking lot of the Black Eagle social club. He spotted the beat-up truck that Burt Garner drove and eased into a spot a few spaces back. Sliding out of his black Tahoe, Danny flipped up the collar on his coat and crossed the parking lot for a quick chat with the host.

Though he belonged to Nikolai Kalasnikov's family, Danny was on good terms with the rival Albanian crew. They handled different pieces of Houston's criminal underworld so there wasn't much competition between them at the moment. He had no problem convincing the host of the social club that doubled as an illegal gambling den to give him the lowdown on Burt.

Once he confirmed that the man had only just arrived, Danny slipped an envelope of cash to the host to buy his neighbor a nice marker and enough credit at the bar to keep him busy for the night and morning. He also pushed a few crisply folded fifties into the host's hand to make sure the transaction was completed without delay. Assured Burt wouldn't be around to bother his family and ruin another Christmas, he returned to his SUV and headed home.

Driving across Houston, Danny thought of Thanksgiving when he had been forced to throw that drunk old bastard onto the street. He had come home from a night guarding a gun shipment for the boss to hear the most terrible sounds of violence coming from the townhouse next door. The police were frequent visitors to the Garner residence yet nothing ever changed.

Rather than rely on them to help, he had beaten on the door until Burt answered and then had dragged the paunchy asshole out onto the front lawn where he had given him a taste of the pummeling the man had just doled out to his family. Frankly, that asshole had been lucky Danny hadn't killed him after he had discovered not only the wife beaten to a bloody pulp but the daughter too.

An arc of pain speared his chest at the memory of Macy's battered face. There were a lot of things Danny had learned to stomach since falling in with Nikolai's crew, but there were lines that should never be crossed. A man did not put his hands on a woman or a child in anger. It wasn't done. Hell, in Nikolai's family, it was a crime punishable by death. The boss didn't fuck around when it came to protecting the vulnerable and neither did Danny.

As he pulled into his parking spot, he acknowledged that his protective instincts toward Macy were growing stronger with every passing day. Since he had crossed paths with her nine months earlier, not one single night went by when he didn't think of her. At first, his interest in the redheaded, blue-eyed beauty had been purely motivated by concern for her welfare. The afternoon he had moved in next door, he had seen the bruises on her arms from being grabbed and jerked around by a much bigger person.

She had been outdoors with her much younger brother and sister when the little boy had crashed his bicycle into Danny's new SUV. He had been pissed off at the dent but had quickly found himself unable to scold the boy or his big sister after he saw the panicked fear in reflected in their eyes. He recognized that look all too well. It was one he had hoped to never inspire.

From that night forward, Danny had vowed to keep an eye on the family next door. The mother was nice enough but haggard and overworked. As best he could tell, she juggled two jobs and relied on Macy to keep up the house and do the bulk of the childcare. The father appeared to work infrequently. What he did make, he pissed away on beer or wasted at the betting tables and on the sports books at the Black Eagle.

It pained Danny to see Macy trapped in her hand-to-mouth existence with that asshole of a father ruining any opportunities she might have to escape. At eighteen, she should have been focused on picking a college and chasing her dreams, not clipping coupons and cooking meals and lugging baskets of laundry between her home and the complex's facilities halfway down the block. He had assumed they had been forced to sell their own washer and dryer set or couldn't afford whatever repairs they needed.

Unlocking his front door, Danny could hear the sounds of two young kids playing and a baby crying next door. The mother had given birth five months ago. He tried not to think about what that woman must go through having that fat, drunk fuck pawing all over her at night. Despite how disgusting Burt was to him, the newest addition to the family, a baby girl named Daisy, was very cute.

Inside his home, Danny tossed his keys into the bowl on the table near the door and loaded up his arms with the gifts he had chosen. Earlier in the week, he had taken the presents to Vivian's studio where she had helped him wrap them. Like everything she touched, Vivi had turned the gifts into works of art with the neatly tied ribbons and hand drawn tags signed in exquisite calligraphy by Santa Claus. Guilt gnawed at him when he thought about how much work Vivi had put into each gift and how quickly the tiny hands next door would rip into and shred the paper.

Feeling a bit giddy inside, Danny carted the gifts to the townhouse where the Garner family lived and stacked them in a sort of pyramid shape atop the welcome mat. Not wanting to have an awkward run-in with the family, he rang the doorbell and ran like hell. Safely inside his house, he pressed his ear to the wall and listened. From the excited cries and laughter, the boxes filled with toys had made two little children very happy.

Pleased with their reaction to his surprise, he slipped out of his jacket, kicked off his shoes, set aside the piece Kostya had given him and filled a kettle with water. The steam was just beginning to whistle through the spout when he heard a knock at his door. He switched off the heat and picked up the pistol, just in case. A quick peek through the peephole assured him that he didn't need it.

After hiding the pistol in the pocket of his jacket, he unlocked and opened his door. Looking anxious and chilled, Macy stood on his welcome mat in just her faded flannel pajama bottoms and a Dallas Cowboys sweatshirt dotted with stains old and new. The oversized top swallowed her small frame and caused a pang of sadness to filter through him. He was hit by the possessive urge to make her his girlfriend so he could shower her with pretty things that had never been cast off from anyone else. He wanted to be able to give her some ease and comfort after such a tough start in life.

"Macy! Come inside. It's freezing." He stepped aside and gestured for her to enter the living room. She seemed hesitant, but a frigid blast of wind convinced her to overcome her hear of being alone with him. He shut the door and asked, "Did you need something?"

"Um, Danny," she said while nervously pushing long strands of that coppery hair behind her ear, "did you leave those gifts at our door?"

"No." He lied with a straight face. "Someone left gifts? Just like that?"

"Yeah." She eyed him suspiciously. "You're sure it wasn't you?"

He laughed. "Macy, I would remember going Christmas shopping." Playing along with the ruse, his brow furrowed. "There weren't any tags on the gifts?"

"They were sent from Santa Claus, apparently." She kept those sky blue eyes narrowed. "If it was you, I just wanted to say thank you." She pinched the worn fabric of her shirt between her fingers and worked it back and forth. "It's been a tight year, with Daisy coming and Dad out of work and Janie taking maternity leave. There, uh, there wasn't much money left over for Christmas so the gifts from Santa Claus mean a lot to Colt and Hannah. Janie started crying when she found the gift cards for gas and groceries." Her gaze remained trained on the floor as she confessed, "The gift cards for books and clothes were something I really wanted too."

His heart ached for her. Not for the first time, he was

tempted to come clean about his feelings and ask her to let him help her. Eighteen and twenty-four weren't too far apart but he knew what people would say. They would think he was taking advantage of her innocence and inexperience. While he doubted she had much practice with men, he recognized that Macy was hardly naïve of the world. She understood how cruel and mean it could be. Now he wanted to be the one to show her how much good there was in it.

What would she say if he asked her on a date? Would she shoot him down instantly or would she indulge her curiosity and say yes? Seeing how skittish she was now, Danny didn't think the latter was very likely. He didn't want her to feel disrespected by offering to take her out, not after he had just given her family all those gifts. He would hate for her to think that was the cost of his generosity.

"I suppose this is just one of those Christmas miracles you hear about this time of year." He shrugged carelessly. "I'm sure the person who sent those gifts just wants to see your brother and sister smile while they play with their new toys."

"You sound pretty sure of that."

"Call it a hunch."

She dragged her teeth along her lower lip. "You can keep up the Secret Santa charade if you want, but I know it was you, Danny. I just…I don't know why."

"Because I like your family," he said matter-of-factly. "Colt and Hannah are nice kids. Your stepmother works hard, and she's got the new baby."

"What about my dad?"

His lips settled into a thin line. "What about your father?"

"You don't like him."

"No, I don't. Do you?" He had often wondered how she felt about the man who treated her so poorly.

"He's my dad. It doesn't matter if I like him or not. I'm stuck with him."

"You're an adult. You could leave."

She scoffed. "And go where? I don't have any other family. The family I do have needs me now. Janie can't work unless I'm here to watch the kids after class. Even if I could figure out a way to get out, what would I do for a job? I still have a semester of high school left. How would I pay for an apartment, a car, insurance and food while finishing school? "

He had that answer. It was simple enough. *Let me take care of you.*

He didn't dare utter the words.

"Did you see my dad tonight?"

Her question threw him. "Why would you ask me that?"

"Because I know what that means," she said, gesturing to the tattoo on his neck.

"Is that so? And what does it mean?"

"It means you run around with that Russian gang."

"I'm a bodyguard. I'm not in a gang."

"Bullshit."

It was the first time he had ever heard anything even close to cursing come out of that pretty mouth of hers. "If you know so much about this tattoo, then you know that I have nothing to do with your father's habits."

"No, that's the Albanians."

An unpleasant sensation invaded his chest. "How do you know about the Albanians?"

"A man came to the house last week looking for dad about a late payment."

"A man? What man?"

"He said his name was Paulie."

Of course. Paulie fought on the underground circuit as Besian's champion and worked enforcement for the loan shark Afrim Barisha. "What else did he say? Did he ask for anything other than money?"

"He offered me a job at his boss' club. He said I could pay off the debt in a few weeks as a waitress there."

Fury burned through him. "The next time Paulie or any of that crew show up at your house, don't open the door. You tell them to come find me, and I'll deal with it. Under no circumstances are you *ever* to go anywhere with Paulie. Do you understand?"

She gulped. "Yes. Why? Is he dangerous?"

"Extremely," he said, certain Paulie would treat her with total disrespect. "Do you know what club he meant?"

"I assumed he meant the social club where Dad gambles."

"No, *milaya moya*." He gently disabused her of that notion. "He meant one of the strip clubs that Besian owns. He meant places like Wet and Sugar's."

"What?" She recoiled with disgust. "Oh, that's gross."

He started to tell her that some women actually enjoyed working in places like that, especially when the money was good, but decided that her reaction was better. It was safer for her to think of the clubs as dens of iniquity. She wouldn't be tempted by promises of big money that way. "Yes, they're terrible places. Awful things happen to the girls who work there. Stay away from those clubs, Macy."

"You don't have to tell me twice. I'll stay away from places like that."

"Good. Be sure that you do."

"I will. I promise."

"I'm holding you to that." *In fact, I wish I was holding you right now.*

A high-pitched wail pierced the wall they shared. She made an apologetic face. "Oh my God, Danny! I had no idea you could hear the kids making that much noise over here! I'll try to keep them quiet from now on."

"Don't even worry about," he hurriedly reassured her. "They're kids. They're supposed to be noisy. If I wanted peace and quiet, I would buy a house. No, I actually like the constant sound. It reminds me of the flat where I grew up."

"Do you ever think about going back?"

"Not as much anymore," he said. "There's nothing for me there."

"No family?"

He shook his head. "The only family I have is here. My uncle is the one who encouraged me to come here when my time in the army was done."

"You were a soldier?"

He nodded. "It's compulsory."

"Oh. I guess you didn't like it well enough to stay in long-term?"

"That life wasn't for me."

"But that one is?" She pointed to his tattoo again.

He ran his fingers over the ink that marked him as part of Nikolai's family. "It's complicated, Macy."

She peered up at him for a long moment. "Someday you'll tell me all about it."

"I doubt that."

"I don't." The baby started to cry again, and Macy sighed. "I need to get back over there. Janie needs me."

"And what about you?" he asked as he followed her to the door. "What do you need, Macy? When do you have time to do what you want?"

"When the kids are a little older, I'll have time to do the things I want to do. Right now, they need me."

She talked like a mother. Danny couldn't explain why her selfless sacrifice impressed him so much. There was such a gentle kindness within her. Even after all the violence and hardship she had known, Macy remained soft-hearted and always ready to give.

But who looked out for her? Who made sure she was getting what she needed?

"Danny?" She gripped the door handle but didn't make a move to open it.

"Yes?"

"You said you like my brother and sisters and my stepmom."

"I do."

"And me?" she asked softly. "Do you like me?'

He swallowed hard. He kept his voice even, lest he reveal too much. "Yes."

"As a friend?"

He tried to read her face. She sounded almost hopeful, but her eyes reflected panic and uncertainty. "Yes, I like you as a friend."

Her smile faltered just the tiniest bit. "Okay."

Cold air swirled around them when she opened the door while he was still trying to process her strange expression. Wondering if this was one of those moments in life where he needed to jump in with both feet, Danny put his hand against the door and shoved it back into place to stop her from escaping just yet. Confused by his action, she glanced up at him. "Danny?"

Taking a cautious step toward Macy, he boxed her in against the door and planted his hands on either side of her head. He was quite a bit taller than her so he had to lean down to reach her mouth. She inhaled a shuddery breath as his lips descended but didn't break eye contact. He waited until the very last second to press his mouth to hers, giving her every possible chance to say no.

Her kittenish whimper sent a jolt of desire through his body. Those small hands of hers flew to his chest, and she gripped his shirt. He nuzzled their noses together for a brief moment before deepening the kiss. Ready to pull back the moment she indicated she didn't want this, he pushed his tongue against the seam of her mouth and sought entrance.

His fucking toes curled against the floor when her soft tongue flicked against his. She slid her arms up his chest to ride the curves of his biceps before finally landing on his shoulders. He wound an arm around her tiny waist and hauled her against his body, wanting to feel the womanly heat of her pressing into him. Tangling his other hand in those gorgeous red waves, he kissed her with all the primal fire of a man finally tasting his personal heaven.

Cock hard and throbbing, he recognized it was time to back off and slow this down. He couldn't have her like this, not tonight. If they were going to pursue a relationship, it had to be done the right way. She deserved to be loved slowly and gently, not lifted up against a door and fucked roughly. No, when it was time, he was going to spend hours lavishing every last millimeter of Macy's body with attention.

He eased off the kiss, ending it with a lingering touch of his lips to hers. They were both breathing hard and trembling when their mouths finally separated. Eyes hazy with lust, Macy gazed up at him so adoringly. A smile curved her swollen pout. "Wow."

He laughed and nestled his nose against her throat. He placed a tender kiss on the spot where her pulse beat so rapidly. "Yes. Wow."

"So…I guess that means you like me as more than a friend."

"It does." He pulled back and peered into her pretty blue eyes. "There's no rush, Macy. My feelings for you don't have a time limit. I know you have a lot going on in your life, and I'm older than you. When you're ready, you come find me."

She ran her finger back and forth along his wrist. "Do you mean that?"

"Yes. Absolutely. You take all the time you need. I'll wait." He kissed her forehead. "Until then, if you need anything, you come to me."

"Okay."

"I mean it, Macy. *Anything.* I'm the man you ask."

"I understand."

"Good." Wanting to kiss her again, he denied himself the pleasure because it would be too damned hard to stop. "You should go."

"Yeah," she said with a breathless smile. "I *really* should."

He stuck his head out the door to watch her leave and make sure she got into her house safely. Lips still buzzing with the intensity of their kiss, he grinned all the way back to the kitchen. He grabbed a box of tea from the pantry and a mug from the shelf. Pouring hot water over a tea bag, he grinned like a fool.

He had been sure that he was on Santa's naughty list but after a magical kiss like that with Macy? Hell, maybe he had squeaked onto the very bottom of the nice list after all!

You can catch up with Danny and Macy in DANILA (Her Russian Protector #9) coming in Summer 2014.

MY FAVORITE THINGS
YURI

Standing back to study the Christmas surprise he had arranged for Lena, Yuri Novakovsky eyed the transformed library with a critical eye. The staff at his Saint Petersburg mansion had outdone themselves to get everything situated while he had taken Lena out for dinner and the ballet. The sketch he had left had been followed exactly with a handful of perfectly chosen glitzy additions from the housekeeper.

Certain Lena would be dazzled by the wintry Christmas wonderland that had popped up in the library, he pulled the silk scarf he had borrowed from her luggage through his hands and smiled. He closed the door behind him and sought out the woman he so passionately loved. Passing Magda in the hall, the housekeeper pointed toward his office and lifted her fingers toward her head in a phone gesture. Understanding, he nodded and quietly wished her a good night.

Easing up to the slightly ajar door, he listened to the conversation happening on the other side. He didn't want to barge in if she was taking an important call. Though it was the holidays, business opportunities waited for no one. He quickly realized she was chatting with her father but still remained in the hallway so she could have some privacy.

After Lena had admitted to her father that her mother was still alive and remarried and not dead as she had told him, Joe had blown up at her. Yuri had been extremely unhappy with her father for behaving so angrily toward Lena and for hurting her even more, but he also tried to understand how Joe must have felt learning the truth after all those years.

He had given the man he hoped would soon be his father-in-law some time to adjust before tracking him down and telling him exactly why Lena had lied as a teenager. He had forced Joe to meet Lena and wouldn't let the duo out of the locked office at his Houston home until they had made peace. There were still some hurt feelings between them, but Yuri was pleased to hear their friendly banter now.

"It's so beautiful here, Dad. I wasn't sure I would like it, but it's nothing like I had imagined. I had this idea that it would be this sad, cold, dreary place but I was so wrong!"

Yuri smiled at her description of Russia. She had in fact been extremely hesitant to come with him to his homeland, but he had persuaded her to give it a try by promising her a whirlwind global tour tacked on to the end of the business trip. Though she hadn't been very impressed by the frigid temperatures when they had landed late at night a week earlier, she had taken a very different view of his country the next morning. Now, she was asking him to stay a few days longer because there were so many places she wanted to see!

"Oh, I don't think you need to worry about that," she said with a laugh. "I have no plans to move here full-time." She paused. "Well, I guess we'll have to cross that bridge when we come to it. No, of course, I don't want to leave Houston forever, but I love Yuri and quite a bit of his business operations are here. Realistically, there's always the possibility that he might ask me to make the move."

Yuri leaned against the wall while she discussed her future with her father. There weren't any easy answers for them. At some point, especially once they were married and had children, the constant travel would wear on them. Depending on the political climate, Yuri might not feel comfortable keeping his family in his homeland. The threats of prosecution for not toeing the party line were a constant worry in the back of his mind. So far he had managed to walk the straight and narrow but he was always ready to bail at a moment's notice.

Then, of course, he had to consider Lena's career. She was only just getting started in the world. Though he wanted to make her his wife and start a family with her, he didn't want that to come at the cost of the education and career she had worked so damned hard to earn and build. A feisty firebrand, Lena held so much possibility. Right now, her future success started in Houston. It was where she needed to be.

So that was where he would stay. Yuri intended to make sure Lena got the chance to go after her dream of having her own crisis PR firm. This winter vacation he had arranged wasn't merely for sightseeing. He intended to massage his vast network of contacts to get her face time with anyone who could offer advice or pointers for the boutique agency she was opening in a few weeks with Ty Weston. Though he wasn't fond of the gossipmongerturned-reputation-and-brand-expert, Yuri grudgingly conceded that Ty knew what he was talking about and had good instincts.

"He took me to the ballet tonight. It was amazing. I can't even find the words to describe it, Dad. The music, the costumes, the dancers—it was extraordinary. I wish you could have been here to see it."

Safe in their private box, Lena had watched the world's finest ballerinas prance and pirouette around the stage with such wonder in her dark eyes. At one point, he had spotted a shiny tear rolling down her cheek. She had been so incredibly moved by the experience. He couldn't wait to take her back again in the spring. Getting her to an opera ranked high on his list of date nights too. She would absolutely love it.

"Did you see Tommy for Christmas? Oh. So he's staying in California then?"

Yuri wasn't surprised to hear that. After the mess her cousin had created with the Guzman cartel, Tommy needed to stay as far away from Houston as possible.

"Oh, he's up to typical Yuri stuff. Working, working, working." She laughed. "Yes, and spoiling me."

He smiled. There was no use in denying any of that.

"He's still doing his physical therapy for his arm and hand. He says he's fine, but I can tell they bother him in the mornings. The weather? I don't know. Maybe…"

He had never bought into the old wives' tales about weather and pain but damned if he wasn't having more problems with the injuries caused by the stabbing he had survived. He hadn't had nearly this amount of discomfort in Houston. Whether it was the Russian cold, he couldn't say.

Knowing Lena could read him so easily amused Yuri. He never wanted to show her any weakness. His male pride demanded he always be the stronger one, but it seemed there were was no way to hide such secrets from Lena. She had offered to give him a massage every morning for the past few days, but he had turned her down in order to make it to meetings on time. Perhaps tomorrow morning he would indulge in a little hands-on help.

"I'm so glad you called. With the time difference, I wasn't sure if I should try to hit you up before we left for the ballet or later tomorrow. Tomorrow we'll video chat, okay? Great. Merry Christmas, Dad. I love you. Bye."

Yuri pushed the door open and made his presence known as she ended her phone call. Still decked out in her formal evening attire, Lena looked like a princess. The light colored gown she wore complemented her warm brown skin to utter perfection. Because he liked her hair down, she had styled the long, black waves in such a way that the front was neatly pinned back while the back flowed loose. He had spent the last half of the ballet performance with his fingers wrapped in those silky tresses.

"How is your father?"

"He's very well. I think our first Christmas apart since he got out of prison might be hitting him hard."

"Would you like to go home? It can be easily arranged."

"No." She left her phone on his desk and crossed the room to join him. She wound her arms around his waist and lifted up to press her lips to his. "This is our first Christmas season together. I don't want it to end yet."

Cupping the back of her neck, he gazed down into her coffee-brown irises. "We don't have to make a decision about where we'll live anytime soon."

She narrowed her eyes at him. "How long were you

skulking out there in the hall?"

"I wouldn't call it skulking. Eavesdropping? Yes." He brushed his mouth against hers. "I didn't want to interrupt you while you were talking to your father. I know things are still tense."

"They're getting better. It will just take time." She rubbed her hand across his chest. "Wherever you are is where I want to be, Yuri. If that's here in Russia, I'll adjust. I'll make it work."

Touched by her willingness to follow him anywhere, he captured her mouth in a loving kiss. "I want to be with you, Lena. For now, Houston is the right place for both of us. I need to come here every few weeks but I don't think I could stand to do my usual two and three week stays."

"Once the business gets off the ground, I'll be able to juggle my schedule. I'm sure I can figure out a way to telecommute."

"We'll figure it out, *lyubimaya moya.*" He nuzzled her cheek. "Are you ready to open your Christmas gifts?"

"Now? But it's so late, and I saw your schedule. You have a meeting—"

He gently silenced her with a finger to her sweet mouth. "It's never too late for me to spoil you." Lifting his hand to reveal the scarf, he commanded, "Turn around for me."

"A blindfold?" She quirked an eyebrow. "Please tell me you haven't been taking gift-giving advice from your kinky friend Niels because this vanilla-sex loving girl isn't interested."

Yuri laughed and applied some pressure to her shoulders. "No, this isn't that sort of gift."

"It better not be." She reluctantly turned around and presented her back to him.

He tied the blindfold in place and put his hands on her hips. Running his hand along the curve of her bottom, he gave her a swat. Lena yelped and rose up on her toes. "As mouthy as you've gotten lately, I'm beginning to see the allure of doling out some discipline."

She pushed back against the hand that had just smacked her backside. "I don't seem to remember you complaining when I was under your desk earlier today and using that mouth of mine to drive you crazy."

His balls ached as he replayed that unbelievably wicked afternoon delight they had shared while he had been taking calls. Sweeping aside her hair, he peppered ticklish kisses along her collarbone and up her neck. "If I remember correctly, I still owe you a return favor for that one."

"Oh, I'm counting on it."

Loving the playful smile curving that sensual mouth of hers, Yuri caressed her face and turned her just enough to kiss her properly. "Come along, sweetheart. I have a surprise for you."

Hand in hand, he guided her down the hallway to the library. Once they were inside, he locked the door behind them because he wanted no interruptions. He swept his gaze around the room one last time to make sure he hadn't missed a thing.

The towers of gifts were arranged around the enormous Christmas tree that Lena had decorated not long after they had arrived in Saint Petersburg. The rug and coffee table near the roaring fire had been replaced with plush, luxurious bedding. A bottle of champagne chilled in an ice bucket on the other side of the room near a light buffet of fruit, cheese and chocolate in case Lena needed a snack before bed.

Carefully untying the blindfold, he pulled it free and

said, "Merry Christmas, kitten."

Her sharp gasp told him he had hit the mark. "Yuri! What did you do?"

"I made some Moscow shopkeepers very, very happy." He massaged her shoulders. "I wanted it to be perfect for you because I know how much you miss your father and your friends."

She spun around and embraced him. "Oh, Yuri, you really know how to make me feel special."

"You are special, Yelena." He kissed the top of her head, drawing the soothing scent of her into his lungs. "You're everything to me."

Leaning back, she gazed up at him with shimmering eyes. "I feel so bad. I only got you a few things."

"Your love is the best gift, the *only* gift, I want." He meant it, and she read the sincerity in his face. "Now," he carefully turned her back around, "before you start tearing into the boxes, there's a rule for tonight."

"Oh?"

"Every time you open a gift, you have to take off a piece of clothing." He slid his hands down her arms. "And, yes, the jewelry you're wearing tonight counts as clothing."

"I see."

"I'm sure you do." He gave her bottom a playful pat. "Go on. Start stripping."

She whirled around and shot him an excited smile before inspecting the gifts. He shucked his tuxedo jacket, kicked off his shoes and removed his cuff links and tie. Flicking through some of the buttons on his shirt, he made his way to the refreshments and opened the champagne. He poured the fizzy liquid into two flutes and handed one to her, then settled onto the wide couch to watch her.

She offered a flirty smile before removing one earring and opening a small box that contained a gold and brilliant green enamel bracelet. Her jaw dropped as she inspected the gorgeous piece. He had an idea that she knew how much a bracelet from that particular designer's line cost, and he waited to hear her protestations. When they didn't come, he was honestly taken aback. She simply smiled at him and slid the bracelet onto her wrist.

Thrilled that she was allowing him to shower her with gifts without complaint, Yuri sipped his champagne. It seemed Lena had finally accepted that he would spend outrageous amounts on her for no other than reason than it pleased him to see her smile. That was all he wanted—to see her smile.

She had been so badly hurt by the mother that had abandoned her. An orphan himself, he understood that empty ache better than anyone else and wanted to help assuage that pain within her. He had given her his heart and showed her how much he loved her and how worthy she was of that love every day. Spoiling her with material things was simply another way to drive home the point that she was someone extraordinary.

Soon Lena had lost both shoes, all of her jewelry and pantyhose. Clad in just a tiny, shiny thong and matching bra, she looked fucking fantastic. Ever the seductress, she didn't disappoint him as she unhooked and slowly removed her bra. He eyed those luscious breasts of hers, the dark nipples forming points that made his mouth water. He couldn't wait to flick his tongue around her velvety skin and make her purr.

"There are so many gifts left, and I'm nearly out of clothes," she said as she picked through the piles. "Which two do you want me to open tonight?"

"That blue box and the small red one over there," he

pointed them out to her. "Bring them over here. Santa wants you to sit on his lap."

"Something tells me that Santa wants me to do a little more than just sit on his lap."

She gathered the two gifts and brought them to the couch. Before she sat down, he grasped the thin side straps on the thong. Grinning wolfishly up at her, he offered, "Let me help you with this."

He pressed his lips to her belly and placed noisy kisses on each thigh as he dragged the scrap of underwear down her legs. He hauled her down on his lap and settled her into place. "Now, open the blue one first."

She did as instructed and discovered the car brochure inside. Gawking at it, she issued a strange noise. "You bought me a car?"

"No, I'm taking you to pick one out when we get back to Houston. A friend of Nikolai's owns several dealerships. We'll visit him and you can test drive anything you want on his lots."

"But my car runs just fine."

"Runs fine? Kitten, the check engine light has been blinking for weeks. If it has a thousand miles left in it, I would be stunned." He set aside the brochure and grazed his fingertips up and down her thigh. "You need a new vehicle, especially if you're going to be meeting clients. You and I both know that what you drive has no bearing on your ability to serve your clients, but appearances are everything in this business."

"I can buy my own car, Yuri."

"I know you can, but I want to do this for you." He traced her lower lip. "If you'll let me," he added hopefully.

"I'll let you go shopping with me."

He sensed there was no way to win this one. While she was getting better at accepting his generosity, it was clear that she was overwhelmed tonight. "Why don't we agree to discuss this when we get back to Houston? We'll figure out a compromise."

"All right. I can live with that."

"Good." He kissed her shoulder. "Open the red one now."

Nervous about her reaction, he slid his arms around her waist and waited anxiously. She untied the silver ribbon and lifted the lid on the box. A quick intake of breath accompanied her discovery of the ring. When she cast panicked eyes on him, he hurriedly sought to explain what it was.

"It's not an engagement ring, Lena. I would elope with you tomorrow morning if I thought you were ready, but I know that you need some time."

Lena's worried expression morphed to one of sheer joy. She examined the ring and ran her fingertip over it. "It's so beautiful Yuri."

"I designed it." He reached for the box and pried loose the ring. A channel of pink diamonds set in rose gold was hugged by two lines of bright white diamonds set in platinum. Reverently, he slipped the ring onto the ring finger of her right hand. "I wanted you to have something that you wear every day that lets everyone else know that you belong to me."

She admired the ring on her finger. "What about you?"

"Kitten, I'll wear anything you give me."

"Anything?"

He considered how mischievous she could be. "Well…within reason."

She wound her arms around his neck and lowered her mouth to his in a tender kiss. "I love you so much, Yuri."

The unopened gifts and the champagne were quickly forgotten as they sought to ease the wild hunger that gripped them. As he sifted his fingers through her hair and plundered her mouth, Lena jerked on the buttons of his shirt and pushed the fabric away from his chest. Her mouth dropped to his nipple. She grazed her teeth across the sensitive nub, making him hiss and buck his hips. She sucked hard, laving her tongue over the stinging spot and making him forget all about that brief discomfort.

His throbbing cock tented the front of his tuxedo trousers. Kissing and nibbling his chest and neck, Lena shifted her position until she straddled his lap. She rocked her bare pussy against the length of his trapped shaft, teasing him with the promise of what was soon to come.

Cupping her bottom with one hand, he slid the other between her thighs and discovered the slick nectar dripping from her core. He craved the taste of her as he penetrated her with one finger and then another, working them into her tight passage while his tongue mimicked his movements, stabbing into her mouth and making her moan.

Unable to deny himself a taste of that pussy he loved so much, he flipped their positions on the couch and dragged her right down to the edge of the cushion. He shoved her thighs open and gazed at the pink, dewy center of her. Lowering his head, he swiped her slit with his pointed tongue, delighting in the cry of pleasure that erupted from her throat. He took his time savoring her cunt, using long, languorous licks to arouse and excite her even more.

Only when she was gripping the cushion did he finally give her exactly what she wanted. He sucked that juicy little berry of a clit between his lips and lavished it with plenty of oral attention. Head thrown back, Lena moaned his name again and again. His dick was so stiff now it hurt so he reached down to free it from this pants. His comfort seen to, he returned all his focus to the woman he loved and that wet, delicious pussy of hers.

"Yuri. *Oh*. Yuri. *Please*."

He groaned against her tender flesh and found a rhythm that was sure to send her flying over the edge. Circling her clitoris, he flicked and fluttered his tongue over it until her toes were curling against his ribs. Her breaths deepened and grew shuddery. Only a little longer now...

"*Yuri!*"

Smiling against her pussy, he forced her thighs even wider apart, splaying her open to him with his elbows and shoulders. He went wild on that tiny bundle of nerves. Tonight, one orgasm wasn't enough. He wanted to her to come and come until she was reduced to a panting, trembling and thoroughly satisfied woman.

"*Yuri!* Oh, God. No more. *No. More.* I can't."

She could. She *would*.

But he took mercy on her, letting her regain her breath as he kissed and caressed her breasts. Her short nails scratched along his scalp, making him shiver in her arms. When their gazes finally met, her eyes still glinted with such arousal and need. Gathering her close, he pulled her down onto the plush bedding that had been arranged and removed the last of his clothes.

Skin to skin, he kissed Lena and glided his hands over her body in a worshipful way. When she pressed on his chest, he understood what she wanted and fell onto his back. He thrust against the warm hand that fondled the length of his shaft. "Let me inside you, Lena."

Grasping the base of his erection, she guided him between the soaking, silky folds of her pussy and pressed him against her entrance. She started to put her hand on his shoulder but remembered his injury and placed it on the pallet instead. Holding his gaze, Lena slowly pushed down on his cock, taking him deep inside the heavenly heat of her.

Exhaling a pent-up breath, Yuri clasped her waist and rocked up into her. They both moaned. Enveloped by the scorching slickness of her pussy, he held her smoky gaze and smiled up at her. She looked so devastatingly beautiful with the firelight dancing across her brown skin. He palmed her breast and brushed his thumb across her nipple as she swayed back and forth.

Gazing up at the gorgeous Latina goddess who had chosen him as the keeper of her heart, Yuri understood how incredibly lucky he had been in life. Every decision he had made, some good and others terrible mistakes, had brought him to this woman, to the love of his life.

Although this Christmas was sweeter than any other in his life, he fully intended to make next year's even better. Filled with hope for the coming year, Yuri thrust up into Lena and tugged her down for a long, heated kiss. By next December, he planned to have his wedding ring on Lena's finger and his child growing in her belly.

A man who thrived on accomplishing his goals, he decided now was a perfect time to practice…

You can read Yuri and Lena's tale in YURI (Her Russian Protector #3) available now in digital and print. The audiobook will be available in early 2014.

FIVE GOLDEN RINGS
IVAN

With Christmas music playing softly in the background, Ivan Markovic sipped some of the sweet and slightly spicy Mexican hot chocolate that Erin loved so much. The woman he intended to claim forever as his own sat cross-legged between his perch on the leather sofa and the Christmas tree she had festively decorated the day after Thanksgiving. His back still twinged from hauling the huge thing inside the house and moving it a dozen different times until it was situated *just* right in front of that window.

The constant adjustments and the four different tree toppers she had insisted he climb the ladder over and over to exchange had frustrated him at the time, but he had experienced only joy when she had wrapped her arms around his waist and grinned up at him. "Our first Christmas tree!" she had said so excitedly.

The words she had used had filled him with the most incredible sense of peace and hope. Yes, their first but far from the last. This morning, he would make sure that they would spend every Christmas for the rest of their lives together.

"Are you ready for another gift?" She took a bite of one of the fluffy, mint-flavored marshmallows from Benny's bakery.

"Yes." He smiled when she clamped the marshmallow between her teeth and moved onto her hands and knees to gather more gifts from under the tree. The red and white striped nightgown she wore rode up on her bottom and gave him a tantalizing flash of thigh. Since Erin had moved in with him earlier in the summer, he had kept to the routine of waking her up every morning with a fantastic romp. This morning, however, she had scampered out of bed before he could snatch her close and slide between her thighs.

"This one is from me." She presented him with a wide, heavy box.

"Another one from you? Erin, how many gifts did you buy me?"

"This is the last one." She glanced at her own pile from him. "Like you should be talking! Look at all this! I'll be opening gifts until Valentine's Day."

He eyed the stack surrounding her. "I might have gone a little overboard, but it is our first Christmas together. It should be special."

She smiled at him and finished eating her marshmallow before opening another gift. He lifted the lid on the box she had given him and found a photo album beneath the tissue paper. While he took another drink of the addictively delicious hot chocolate, he curiously flipped the cover of the album, turned the first two blank pages—and promptly choked on the hot, sweet liquid in his mouth.

There, in black and white, was an erotic photograph of Erin. Flat on her back atop a silky sheet, she wore skimpy lace lingerie and playfully teethed the strand of pearls he had gifted her a few months earlier. The photographer had highlighted the ribbon accents of her lingerie with hot pink pops of color.

Swallowing hard, he glanced over at the little vixen who had ensnared him the day she had bravely entered his gym and asked for his help. She nibbled another marshmallow and eyed him with amusement. "Do you like it?"

"You should have warned me before I opened this box. I nearly choked to death."

She giggled. "So I'll take that as a yes."

"Yes, *angel moy*, I like it very much." He turned the page to find her in the same lingerie but in an even more provocative pose. "Please tell me you still have this lingerie."

She snorted with amusement. "I do. All three sets from the album are hidden upstairs. I thought I would let you choose which one I wear first."

Turning the pages and becoming increasingly more aroused, he had a troubling thought. Clearing his throat, he asked, "Where did you take these?"

She grinned playfully. "Guess."

He narrowed his eyes. Jealousy burned through him at the idea of another man seeing her this way. "Was it a man? Because if it was—"

She rolled her eyes at his possessiveness. "It was Vivian."

He blinked. "Vivian?"

"Yep. Vivian."

He considered the young woman who waited tables at Samovar and seemed so completely innocent. Could a woman like that understand such sensuality? "I don't believe it."

"Lena and Benny helped style the shoot, but Vivian was the one who sketched out the ideas, took the photographs and did all the editing to make each photo so beautiful. I told her that she should consider offering boudoir shoots as a side business."

Ivan couldn't help but wonder what Nikolai would think of that. "The copies of these photos?"

"They're on a flash drive in your office safe. Vivian did all the printing in her studio so we're the only ones who have seen them."

The jealousy within him faded. "Have I upset you?"

She laughed. "No, baby, I've gotten used to this alpha male thing you do."

Loving the way she called him baby, he let his gaze fall back to the erotic photos. The fireplace crackled, and Erin pushed up off the ground. She grabbed another log from the stack he had carried in the day prior.

"Careful, *milaya moya*," he urged, worried she would burn herself.

"Ivan," she said with an exasperated laugh, "I'm a big girl. I can handle adding a log to a fire."

"I know." But his protectiveness toward her would never fade. He thought of recent discussions he had shared with Dimitri as his friend prepared for the birth of his first child. When it was time for him to make a baby with Erin, would the same fears beset him? Undoubtedly yes.

Her chore finished, she returned to her spot on the floor and continued unwrapping gifts. "We'll need more wood brought inside if you plan to keep the fires going here and in our bedroom tonight."

"I'll take care of it after lunch."

"Are you going to use the ax again?"

He heard the hopefulness in her voice and smiled. "Some of the wood will probably have to be cut down, yes."

"Please tell me you're going to wear that sexy flannel shirt again."

He still couldn't believe how easily she was aroused by him doing manly things like fighting or chopping wood. "Of course, *angel moy*. Whatever you want...as long as I get what I want when I'm finished."

"Ivan, I'm probably going to get so hot watching you act like a big, sexy man beast that you'll be lucky to get inside the back door before I'm riding you like a cowgirl."

Heat flared in his lower belly as the image of Erin bouncing on his cock flashed before him. Seemingly oblivious to the way she affected him, Erin continued opening gifts. He thumbed through the album and set it aside to look at the other gifts she had given him. While he scanned a new book, she began to pick up the mess they had made, stuffing the scraps of paper and ribbon into a trash bag that she had fetched from the kitchen.

Ivan's mouth went dry as he recognized the moment was upon him. Though he had been planning and playing out this scenario for weeks, his courage fled. What if he was wrong? What if Erin wasn't ready to be a wife? Or worse. What if she didn't want to be *his* wife?

Those old doubts crept up on him. Despite his successes in business and life, he feared he wasn't good enough for her. The sins of his time in the mob would never truly leave him. The tattoos marking his skin were a constant reminder of those dark deeds.

The sweet, gentleness of Erin had soothed the beast within him. She made him want to be a better man. For her, he would do anything. For the chance to build a family with her, he would give anything.

Heart racing and fingers trembling, Ivan waited for Erin to come close to the couch. "Angel, you missed a piece."

She crawled toward him. "Did I?"

He lifted the piece of wrapping paper he had earlier arranged and revealed the box hidden underneath. Erin eyed him suspiciously and reached for the box. She gasped when she noticed the four simple but beautiful rings in rose, white and yellow gold he had tied onto the decorative ribbons and bow. "Ivan?"

"I wanted to get you some jewelry. That Christmas carol talks about giving your true love five golden rings so I thought why not?"

"But there are only four golden rings on here," she said, touching each one.

"Open the box, Erin." His heart beat so rapidly now he had a hard time breathing.

She did as instructed—and sucked in a shocked breath. She gazed upon the engagement ring nestled inside the box for a long moment. When she finally met his questioning gaze, he took the box from her hand and removed the ring he had designed for her. It was a big, brilliant round diamond surrounded by dozens of tiny diamonds set in a delicate gold band with exquisite scrollwork accents. He couldn't wait to see it on her finger.

"Come here." He didn't think proposing while she knelt at his feet was right. He wanted her to be his partner in life, not his servant. Sliding his arm around her waist, he hauled her onto his lap and peered into her beautiful eyes. "I love you, Erin. I didn't even know if it was possible for me to feel this way until you. You were the first for me—and the last. It's you I want. Only you."

She placed her small hand against his jaw. Her eyes shone with unshed tears. "Ask me, Ivan."

"Marry me, Erin? Build a life with me, *angel moy*."

"Yes." Her lower lip trembled, and she threw her arms around his neck. Pressing her face into the curve of his throat, she let loose a little sob and whispered, "Oh, Ivan, I love you so much."

"I love you, *angel moy*." He wrapped his arms around her and tried not to squeeze her too tightly. His heart threatened to burst with joy. "I'll make you happy, Erin."

"You already make me happy."

"We'll have a good life together. I promise you that."

"I know we will." She leaned back and caressed his face. He grasped her hand and dragged it down so he could slide the ring onto her dainty finger. "It's so pretty."

"You like it?"

"So much," she assured him. "It's perfect."

He pushed her bangs back and nuzzled their noses together. "Kiss me, Erin."

She tenderly touched her lips to his. The barest brush of her mouth was like a spark to dry tender. His lust ignited, Ivan deepened their kiss, relishing the sweet, minty hint of the marshmallow that clung to her tongue. Whimpering, she clutched at him and broke their kiss. "Take me upstairs, Ivan. Make love to me."

Standing up with her cradled safely in his arms, he kicked aside the wrapping paper in his way and carried her across the living room and upstairs. There were times when being a big, strong man was incredibly useful—and this was one of them.

When he reached their bedroom, he gently placed her on the bed. Mouths mating, they tore at each other's clothes and were soon naked. Flushed with the heat of desire, her blazing hot skin seared his. Ivan reined in the raging need to ravish her and chose instead to take his time loving her. Now that she would be his forever, there was no need to rush.

Propped up on his elbow, he claimed her lips in an endless series of kisses and ran his palm over her breasts and belly. Though her thighs fell open in silent invitation, he held off touching her so intimately. He marveled at the sight of his larger, rough-looking hand moving over her supple skin. His tattooed fingers and gnarled, busted knuckles were so harsh compared to the smooth expanse of her unmarked skin. When she entwined her fingers with his, he understood how oddly matched they were—and yet how perfectly she balanced him.

Erin cupped the back of his head, scratching her nails over his scalp, and arched into him. Her stiff nipples grazed his chest and reminded him how much he loved tormenting them. Dropping his head, he circled the pink flesh with his tongue before suckling her. He bit down gently, just enough to make her hiss, and then soothed the reddened peaks with his tongue. She cried out with pleasure and bucked against him, urging him on with her rapturous sounds.

When both of her nipples were wet and puckered, he returned to her mouth, tasting her and loving every moment of it. His hand finally found its way between her thighs. He probed her carefully and with the utmost gentleness. Hot and slick, she responded so sweetly to his ministrations. He strummed her clit with a pace that was meant to arouse but not bring her to a climax.

Wanting to touch him, she slid her hand down between their bodies and stroked his cock from the very tip to the base and back up again. Already he was leaking pre-cum and dying to bury himself in her snug pussy. Erin's hand slid even farther down to cup his sac, causing him to groan as she fondled him so expertly. Her other hand clutched at his thigh, her nails biting into his skin, and she flicked her tongue against his lower lip.

"Now, Ivan," she begged. "I need you now."

He shifted until he was between her thighs, and she wrapped her shapely legs around his waist. Still holding his cock in her small hand, she pushed him through the pink petals of her sex until he was perfectly aligned. With one fluid thrust, he sheathed himself in the welcoming heat of her. Touching his forehead to hers, Ivan retreated until only the tip of him was buried in her before thrusting forward again.

They writhed atop the bed, their passionate coupling growing more frenzied with each passing minute. He nipped at her neck, marking her with his teeth. He loved the way her pussy fluttered around him, clenching and squeezing him with every love bite. Rubbing her clitoris, he drove his cock into her again and again. "Come with me, Erin. Come for me, *angel moy.*"

Crying out, she found her release in his arms. The spasms of her pussy pushed him right up to the edge. Still panting and shuddering, Erin clung to his shoulders and gazed up at him with such love in her eyes. His entire future was reflected in those green irises. Heart swelling in his chest, he punctuated every thrust of his hips with a sweetly whispered, "I love you."

Holding him close, Erin returned his whispers of love and urged him on toward his climax. Trying to draw it out, he focused on her beautiful face and captured her lips. He hovered just on the edge for a moment before finally surrendering to the blissful heat gripping his core.

Sliding deep, he spilled his seed, all the while wishing for the day it would take hold in Erin's womb. She had shown him how wonderful life could be when he had someone to love, spoil and protect. He yearned for the day when their house would be filled with the sounds of their children.

Resting his head against her breast, Ivan repositioned the weight of his body just to the side of her and embraced her waist. He listened to the fast beat of her heart and tried to fight the sleepy pull that always hit him after they made love. Erin's soft hand petting his head didn't help. "You're going to put me to sleep."

"So?"

"So we have things to do."

"Like?"

Suddenly, he couldn't think of anything.

"It's Christmas, and we've just gotten engaged. As far as I'm concerned, there's no reason to get out of bed today."

He kissed her breast. "That's a tempting idea."

"It's the best idea." She wiggled a little and found a more comfortable position. "Pull up the covers, baby. I'm freezing."

He reached down, grabbed the fluffy comforter she had chosen for their bed and dragged it over their rapidly cooling bodies. "I've got a few ideas for keeping you warm."

She giggled and snuggled into him. "Just for today?"

"No," he kissed her lovingly. "I'll keep you warm always, *angel moy*."

You can read Ivan and Erin's story in IVAN (Her Russian Protector #1) available now in ebook (for FREE at all retailers,) in print and in audiobook. There a number of free reads featuring the pair available at my website.

A BRIGHT NEW BEGINNING
SERGEI

The night after Christmas, Sergei Sakharov leaned back against a wall, crossed his arms and kept a close eye on Vivian Valero. All around him, the VIP guests at Houston's hottest nightspot milled and jostled. Tonight, Faze was on fire. Yuri Novakovsky, the Russian oligarch who owned the club, had discovered the perfect mix of ambience, music and drink specials to keep the bouncers out front busy.

While he wasn't thrilled with his glorified babysitting duties, Sergei understood that the job had been given to him because Nikolai trusted him without reservation. The boss had made it perfectly clear that the threat to Vivian was very real and extremely dangerous. With her father out of the pen on early release and in the custody of the U.S. Marshals, it was only a matter of time before her old man's outlaw motorcycle crew or the hit squad from the Guzman cartel came calling.

Scanning the VIP section, Sergei made note of the two men coming up the stairs. The bouncer stationed at the entrance to the exclusive enclave checked the men over before letting them pass. Sergei gave them a thorough once-over before turning his attention back to Vivian. Here, surrounded by athletes, musicians and Houston's trust fund babies, she was relatively safe. Neither the motorcycle club nor the cartel would ever dare to touch her where there were so many witnesses.

Later, when they were alone in his SUV, an attack was within the realm of possibility. Three-Fingered Arty and his small crew of soldiers had shadowed them tonight. Sergei remained in contact with the captain via text message. When it was time to leave, Arty and his men would follow a few car lengths behind, just in case. Nikolai didn't want Vivian upset or worried by a heavy presence of guards so he had arranged a low-profile escort to ensure the right amount of manpower was available if the worst happened.

Certain Vivian was safe for now, Sergei allowed his gaze to slide over to that staggeringly gorgeous friend of hers. *Bianca Bradshaw.* He committed her name to memory and tried to burn the details of her into his mind. This was a woman who would star in his dreams and fantasies.

The dark-skinned beauty laughed as she waited near the bar for another cocktail. Her warm brown skin and curly hair called to him. He had never dated a girl like Bianca. Blondes and redheads had always been his go-to type, but when Bianca had entered the restaurant earlier that evening, he had become instantly aware of her. Even before he had learned she was Vivian's friend, he had been planning to introduce himself and chat her up. Bianca was one-of-a-kind, and he hoped to get to know her very well.

His stomach somersaulted when she glanced his way and flashed him a pretty smile. That deep berry lipstick she wore had just a little shine to it. He couldn't stop looking at that pouty, sensual mouth of hers and wondering what it would be like to kiss her. One kiss wouldn't be enough. He sensed she would be utterly intoxicating.

His gaze roamed her lush body. She wasn't very tall, but she had a thick body that provoked such a strong, lustful response. That gold dress hugged her curves so perfectly, highlighting her generous breasts and an ass that made him want to drop to his knees so he could worship her the way she deserved. He couldn't help but imagine her naked in his bed. Would she purr when he stroked between her thighs? Would she cry out his name when he thrust deep into the slick feminine core of her?

Eyes closing briefly, he could almost feel her wet, hot pussy squeezing his cock. Face hot and ears burning, Sergei tried to get a fucking grip. His surprising reaction to Bianca stunned him. With his larger-than-normal size and good looks, he had never had a problem finding a date. Women came onto him constantly—but none of them made him feel like this.

A couple of guys who weren't part of the larger group of Vivian's friends came over to ask the two women to dance. Nikolai hadn't given him any orders about keeping other men from touching Vivian, but he figured the boss wouldn't want anyone grinding up against her. Though Nikolai had never come right out and admitted that he was sweet on Vivian, it was clear to anyone who watched them in private moments that love existed between the pair.

Sergei shadowed the two women down to the main floor, just in case. Besides, that blond-haired prick with his hand on Bianca's back would do well to keep it there. If the other man dared to let that hand slide any lower,

Sergei wasn't sure he would be able to control himself. Jealousy darted through his gut, and he had to flex his fingers at his sides to keep it in check.

Watching Bianca dance with the other man nearly drove him insane. She moved with such lithe grace. Unlike some of the women around her who were rocking against their dates in the most outrageous ways, Bianca kept a respectable amount of distance between her and the man who had asked her to dance. The guy tried to rub up against her ass once, but she shook her head and gave him a slight shove back.

Sergei's mouth curved with a proud smile at the way she enforced her personal boundaries. He liked a strong woman, and Bianca definitely fit that description. Classy, beautiful and independent, she was exactly the sort of woman he wanted.

During the night, he had overhead enough of her conversations with Vivian to know that Bianca was so far out of his league that he had absolutely no chance with her—but he couldn't kill the hope clinging to life within him. She ran her family's wedding boutique, designed bridal gowns and had attended one of the most prestigious fashion schools in the world. In stark contrast, Sergei now worked as an enforcer for a mob boss and fought in the underground bare-knuckle tournaments for the crime family that owned him.

A glimmer of resentment rippled through him as he considered how life might have been different if his older brother hadn't fucked things up so massively. He wouldn't be indebted to the Prokhorov crime family. He wouldn't be forced to pay off his debts by fighting and enforcing and doing all the terrible things that Nikolai required of him. He could have been an architect instead of taking a cut of one of the legit construction businesses his boss owned.

But if his brother hadn't done those stupid things, Sergei wouldn't have been here in Houston, and he never would have crossed paths with Bianca Bradshaw.

Conflicted and wondering what the future held in store for him, Sergei watched the guy dancing with Vivian. He recognized the way the man was trying to separate her from Bianca. Sergei had used a similar move many times in the past when he was dancing with a woman who was giving him all the right signals, but Vivian wasn't giving out those signals. She offered her dance partner a timid smile and tried to move closer to Bianca, but the man blocked her attempt and edged her back toward a dark corner.

Sergei hesitated only long enough to see if Vivian could handle the situation herself. While the boss was incredibly protective of her, Sergei chose to give her some space whenever possible.

Right now, it wasn't possible. She put both hands on the guy's chest, but he wouldn't budge. When he swooped down to kiss her, Vivian turned her head—and Sergei pounced. Gripping the man's shoulder, he spun him around and gave the creep a slight shove. "She said no."

The guy sized him up and smartly decided not to push his luck. "Yeah. Okay." He held up both hands and shrugged at Vivian. "Sorry. I thought we had something going."

"It's okay." She offered him a smile, and the guy disappeared into the crowd.

Sergei bent down so he wouldn't have to shout at her. "Are you okay?"

"Yeah. Thank you. I just—um—I guess I was sending out the wrong signals."

"I think your signals were clear. His radar is fucked."

Grinning, she patted his arm before taking Bianca's outstretched hand and following her friend back up to the VIP area. The blond who had been dancing with Bianca started to follow, but Sergei put his hand on the man's chest and shook his head. "Find some other girls. These two are mine."

They weren't, but the blond didn't know that and he sure as hell didn't question it. Back upstairs with Vivian and Bianca, Sergei made sure they were comfortable and surrounded by their friends before taking up a position between the main access point and the woman he had promised to protect. The night continued without another incident. The girls danced, had a few drinks and chatted with their friends.

After a fight broke out on the dance floor, Sergei decided it was time to get Vivian and her friend home. He grabbed their coats and purses from their hostess and approached the two women with a no-nonsense look on his face to discourage any whining or attempts at manipulating him to let them stay longer.

"Okay, ladies, it's time to go."

Vivian sighed dramatically and snatched her purse from him. "Fine."

He tucked Bianca's purse and coat under his arm and helped Vivian into hers. When he shook out Bianca's coat, she gave him a strange look but turned her back and let him drape it across her shoulders. She was so close now that he caught the delicious scent wafting from her. He inhaled her flirty, feminine smell and tried to memorize the faint notes of it.

As soon as her arms were through the sleeves, Bianca hastily moved away from him and shot him a wary look. The unease in her dark eyes cut him deeply. While he wasn't employed in the most respectable way, he wasn't a bad person. He hated that she judged him for *what* he was instead of *who* he was.

Ignoring the pain of her rejection, he flicked his fingers. "Come on. I'll drive you home."

Bianca shook her head. "I'll get a cab.

He wasn't about to let her take a taxi. Anything could happen to her if she was alone in some strange man's car. "It's cold and late. You'll come with us."

Upon hearing his order, Bianca cast a look Vivian's way. "Are they always bossy like this?"

Vivian smiled up at him. "He's pretty tame compared to some others."

In fact, Vivian was dead wrong. The dominant, alpha streak within him was one he had tried to suppress as a younger man but one he fully embraced now. He understood that his need to care for his woman, to protect her and provide for her, was as innately necessary to him as breathing.

Bianca tugged her purse from his grasp. "Well—let's go Hulk. Take me home."

Oh, he wanted to do more than just take her home. He started to come onto her but thought better of it. Something told him she wouldn't appreciate it. Bianca was the sort of woman who required a more subtle approach.

With his wide shoulders and intimidating size, he led the women through the crowd and out of the club. He helped them inside his SUV, Vivian in the front passenger seat and Bianca in the row behind her friend. He blasted the heater for them and switched on the windshield wipers as a misty haze of wintry precipitation began to fall.

As they pulled out of the Faze parking lot, Vivian typed Bianca's address into the GPS. Later, when he was alone, he would write it down and slip the paper into his wallet. He acknowledged the move verged on stalker territory, but he wanted to know everything about this girl. He recognized the area on the map. It was a historical section of the city not far from the mansion that Nikolai had restored.

The light haze turned to a drizzle. Mindful of the nasty weather and his precious cargo, Sergei drove carefully. When his phone started to ring, he tugged it out of his pocket, but Vivian swiped it. He tried to snatch it back, but she slapped his hand. "You can't talk and drive!"

"Children, do we need to pull over?" Bianca asked from the backseat, her voice laced with amusement.

He glanced at her reflection in the rear view mirror. Her infectious smile made his heart do a wild flip. God, what he wouldn't give to see that smile peeking up at him every morning when he rolled over in bed.

"Hello?" Vivian answered his phone and instantly switched to Russian. "Calm down. He's driving. We're taking my friend home."

Sergei could just make out the sound of Nikolai's voice. The boss sounded aggravated. That didn't bode well for his night.

"What's wrong?" Vivian listened intently and spoke softly. "It's not your fault."

Not his fault? What in the hell had happened now?

"I'll see you in fifteen minutes or so." She ended the call and met his questioning gaze. "Someone vandalized my studio. Nikolai wants you to bring me there."

Sergei tightened his grip on the steering wheel. He had been hoping to get a good night's rest before heading to the gym but he had a bad feeling he was going to be up all night—and not in the way he enjoyed best. No doubt, his fists would be called into service by the boss. "Yeah.

Okay."

Bianca leaned forward. "Um, what's going on?" She pointed to herself. "Doesn't speak Russian, remember?"

Sergei felt bad that he had forgotten Bianca couldn't understand. Vivian smiled apologetically at her friend. "Sorry! There was some vandalism at my studio."

"Oh no! What about your paintings? Oh, I hope they're all okay. Do you want me to come with you?"

He liked the way Bianca instantly supported her friend. Her loyalty and concern showed what a kind heart she possessed.

"No, this is probably going to keep me up all night. You have brides coming for their last-minute fittings tomorrow." Vivian reached back and squeezed her friend's hand. "But I really appreciate the offer."

In no time at all, they were driving down Bianca's street. He pulled up in front of her house and cast a scrutinizing gaze toward the Queen Anne. Even in the dark, he could tell the house needed a new roof. He assumed the paint looked pretty bad in the light of day. The cosmetic issues aside, the home seemed to be in pretty solid shape.

He unlatched his seatbelt and pointed a finger at Vivian. "You sit here. I'll be right back."

Not giving Bianca a chance to protest, he grabbed the umbrella he kept tucked into the compartment on the door and slid out of his seat. He popped open the umbrella, walked around his vehicle and opened Bianca's door. When he held out his hand, she stared at it for a few seconds before she finally placed her palm against his.

Like a jolt of electricity, her touch enlivened every nerve-ending in his body. Intensely aware of the lush woman next to him, Sergei ensured she was completely covered by the umbrella's wide canopy on their trek down her sidewalk. Covered by the porch, he lowered the umbrella and waited for her to find her keys.

"Do you want me to go inside and check the house?"

She glanced back at him and frowned. "Why in the world would you need to check my house?"

"It's late. It's dark. You're a woman who lives alone." He ticked off the reasons why she would make an easy target.

"No, thank you. I'm fine."

"You should get a security system or a dog." He didn't like the thought of her living alone in such a big house. A neighborhood like this one was prime burglary territory. "Do you have a concealed handgun permit?"

"Are you crazy?" She pushed open her door and stepped inside, flicking on the entryway light. "Do I look like the sort of girl who packs a pistol in her purse?"

Seizing his opening, he said, "You look like the sort of girl I would like to take out sometime."

Bianca blinked a few times and then laughed. "Yeah, that's not going to happen."

Bristling at her rejection, he asked, "Why not?"

She leveled a stare at him. "You know why."

"I don't."

"Um, okay, how about a guy named Nikolai Kalasnikov? That ring any bells?"

"You mean your best friend's boss and guardian? That Nikolai?"

She pursed those berry-colored lips at the way he had so easily pointed out her hypocrisy. "That's different."

"Because?"

"Because Vivi doesn't do the things you do."

"And what is it that I do?"

She shrugged. "You know…illegal stuff."

"Like?" He wondered what she thought he did all day.

"I don't know," she admitted.

"One date," he said, lifting a thick finger. "Let me take you out once. You won't be disappointed."

She swallowed, almost as if wavering, and parted her lips to answer him. Before she got a word out, she clamped them shut, clearly changing her mind, and shook her head. "No. I'm flattered, Sergei, but I don't date men like you."

Her words slashed at him like a razor. She must have seen the flash of pain they caused because she reached out and brushed her fingertips along his hand. "I didn't mean it to sound so ugly. From what I've seen, you're a really nice man, Sergei. Honestly, I don't get why you're all mixed up in Nikolai's family."

"It's a long story, sweetheart."

One side of her mouth lifted with amusement at his pet name. He expected her to verbally smack him for calling her sweetheart, but she let it go. Giving his chest a gentle pat, she said, "Sergei, there are lines I don't cross. The mob? That's one of them." She backed into the entryway. "Good night, Sergei. Thank you for bringing me home."

"Anytime." He gestured toward her house. "The next time you need some work done, get my number from Vivian. I can send a crew out here."

She seemed surprised by his offer. "Thank you. I'll think about it."

She would think about it, but she wasn't going to call. He sensed Bianca Bradshaw had a stubborn streak in her a mile wide.

"Night." She pushed the door closed.

"Good night, Bianca." He waited until he heard the locks engaging before returning to the idling SUV.

Spotting Arty's sedan halfway down the block, he slid behind the wheel and ignored Vivian's curious stare. He didn't want to talk about his interest in her friend. She would probably have a list ten pages long about why it wouldn't work. He was already working on a list eleven pages long about how it would.

Not an easily discouraged man, Sergei thought of Bianca as he navigated the slick Houston streets. She might have shot him down, but he had seen the interest in her gorgeous eyes. He had also caught a glimpse of something else in them—fear. There was a story there, something that made her afraid of getting involved with him, and he meant to uncover it.

Certain that Bianca was a special woman, the kind who came into a man's life once and only once, Sergei accepted the challenge of wooing her. It might take weeks or months, but he was determined to show her that he was worth more as a man than his criminal connections. She was worth the effort.

Turning down the street where Vivian's studio was located, Sergei let himself feel a bit of excitement before that hard, harsh mask he wore on the job was forced back into place. He had something new and wonderful in his life now, something clean and pure and not of this dark underworld he was forced to inhabit. He had a reason to fight his way out now—a woman who deserved a man she could be proud of on her arm.

Yes. Sergei suspected the coming year was going to be very interesting indeed.

You can read all about Sergei and Bianca in SERGEI (Her Russian Protector #5) available now in ebook and print. A sequel to their novel, SERGEI, Volume 2, will be released in Spring 2014.

AUTHOR'S NOTE

Thanks so much for reading A Very Russian Christmas. I hope you enjoyed revisiting old couples and discovering new ones. The next books in the series will release in 2014 and include two sequels—NIKOLAI, Volume 2 (*Her Russian Protector #6*) and SERGEI, Volume 2 (*Her Russian Protector #5.5*)—and KOSTYA (*Her Russian Protector #7*), ALEXEI (*Her Russian Protector #8*) and DANILA (*Her Russian Protecor #9.*)

You can check out my website, Facebook page or sign up for my newsletter for updates and notices on upcoming releases. I also offer Free Reads featuring couples from my books on my website.

ABOUT THE AUTHOR

When I'm not chasing after my wild preschooler, I like to write super sexy romances and scorching hot erotica. I live in Texas with a husband who could easily snag a job as an extra on History Channel's new Viking series and a sweet but rowdy four-year-old.

I also have another dirty-book writing alter ego, Lolita Lopez, who writes deliciously steamy tales for Ellora's Cave, Forever Yours/Grand Central, Mischief/Harper Collins UK, Siren Publishing and Cleis Press.

You can find me online at www.roxierivera.com.

ROXIE'S BACKLIST

<u>Her Russian Protector Series</u>
Ivan (Her Russian Protector #1)
Dimitri (Her Russian Protector #2)
Yuri (Her Russian Protector #3)
Nikolai (Her Russian Protector #4)
Sergei (Her Russian Protector #5
Nikolai Volume 2 (Coming 2014)
Sergei Volume 2 (Coming 2014)
Kostya (Coming 2014)
Alexei (Coming 2014)
Danila (Coming 2014)

<u>The Fighting Connollys Series</u>
In Kelly's Corner (Fighting Connollys #1)
In Jack's Arms (Fighting Connollys #2)—Coming January 2014!
In Finn's Heart (Fighting Connollys #3)—Coming March 2014!

<u>Seduced By…</u>
Seduced by the Loan Shark
Seduced by the Loan Shark 2—Coming Soon!
Seduced by the Congressman
Seduced by the Congressman 2

<u>Erotica</u>
Chance's Bad, Bad Girl
Halftime With Craig
Tease
Eddie's Cuffs 1
Eddie's Cuffs 2
Eddie's Cuffs 3
Disturbing the Peace
Quid Pro Quo
Search and Seizure

A Very Russian Christmas

www.ingramcontent.com/pod-product-compliance
Lightning Source LLC
Chambersburg PA
CBHW020246150626
46552CB00020B/427